Run Away Home

The Loves of Lakeside

Run Away Home

MIMI FRANCIS

4 Horsemen
Publications, Inc.

Run Away Home
Copyright © 2021 Mimi Francis. All rights reserved.

4 Horsemen
Publications, Inc.

4 Horsemen Publications, Inc.
1497 Main St. Suite 169
Dunedin, FL 34698
4horsemenpublications.com
info@4horsemenpublications.com

Cover by Battle Goddess Productions
Typeset by Michelle Cline
Editor JM Paquette

All rights to the work within are reserved to the author and publisher. No part of this publication may be reproduced, stored in a retrieval system, or transmitted in any form or by any means, electronic, mechanical, photocopying, recording, scanning, or otherwise, except as permitted under Section 107 or 108 of the 1976 International Copyright Act, without prior written permission except in brief quotations embodied in critical articles and reviews. Please contact either the Publisher or Author to gain permission.

This is book is meant as a reference guide. All characters, organizations, and events portrayed in this novel are either products of the author's imagination or are used fictitiously. All brands, quotes, and cited work respectfully belongs to the original rights holders and bear no affiliation to the authors or publisher.

Library of Congress Control Number: 2021938970

Print ISBN: 978-1-64450-220-4
Audio ISBN: 978-1-64450-218-1
Ebook ISBN: 978-1-64450-219-8

Table of Contents

Chapter One Serena 1
Chapter Two Van 11
Chapter Three Serena 19
Chapter Four Van 27
Chapter Five Serena 39
Chapter Six Van 51
Chapter Seven Serena 61
Chapter Eight Van 71
Chapter Nine Serena 81
Chapter Ten Van 91
Chapter Eleven Serena 101
Chapter Twelve Van 109
Epilogue 117

Chapter One
Serena

Force of habit made her check her surroundings before she shoved open the car door. No one was around, not in this neighborhood on a late September evening. Deserted condos lined the lake this time of year. Most of these were summer homes, occupied only during the warm Montana summers.

Serena pushed the car door closed, put her arms over her head and stretched, working out the kinks in her back from the eighteen-hour drive. The scent of fresh rain washed over her. She took a deep breath; after years of living in smog-riddled Los Angeles and its kissing cousin, Phoenix, she'd forgotten how wonderful the air in Montana smelled. It dredged up memories of barbecues, swimming in the lake, boat rides to the islands dotting Flathead, and antiquing with her parents.

Happier times, better times. She closed her eyes, a smile dancing across her lips, and breathed it in. It was good to be home.

Serena turned in a circle, re-familiarizing herself with the area. She froze when her eyes met those of a tall, muscular, brown-haired stranger leaning on the balcony railing of the condo across the way, a mug in his hand, steam rising from it. A scowl marred his handsome features as he took her in, then he pivoted and went inside.

"What the hell?" she muttered under her breath. She didn't recognize him; not that she would since it had been years since she'd been here. Her father might know who he was. She'd have to ask him when they talked.

She unloaded the car and dragged her meager belongings inside, pushing the stranger and his angry scowl out of her head. She'd had enough of men and their disdain for women. She tossed everything in the bedroom and peeled off her clothes. Before she did anything else, she needed to wash the last two days from her skin, along with Arizona and Trace.

Serena found a bar of soap and some hotel shampoo and conditioner in one of the bathroom drawers while she waited for the water to warm up. She stood under the shower head, shivering as the lukewarm water washed over her. She'd grown accustomed to the Arizona heat. It was going to take some time to get used to the cold.

She held the tears at bay until she cleaned herself up, then she sank to the bottom of the bathtub as sobs wracked her body, bending her in half, tearing out of her like she was expelling a demon.

A demon named Trace.

— *Serena* —

She stayed on the bottom of the tub until the water ran cold and the shivers tore through her, then she shut off the shower and stepped onto the tile floor. The towels were under the sink, beneath the room-length mirror.

The bruises stood out in stark contrast to her pale skin, the harsh fluorescent lights of the bathroom making the purple, blue, and yellow marks look worse than she'd thought—one in the shape of a handprint on her upper arm, another on her wrist, several on her thighs, and the worst of them, a huge blood red oval shaped bruise on her side where she'd run into the door.

Serena turned her back on the mirror, snatched a towel off the top of the pile, and wrapped it around herself, then she threw open the bathroom door and stumbled across the hall to the bedroom. She yanked some clothes out of her bag, pulled them on, and dropped to the end of the bed, her head in her hands.

Droplets of water hit the floor between her legs and her wet hair clung to the back of her neck. She shuddered, her entire body succumbing to the emotions racing through her. Every muscle in her body ached, her eyes burned, and her throat felt like she'd swallowed grains of sand. Exhaustion held her hostage, weighing her down.

She towel-dried her hair, used her fingers to comb it, and pushed it out of her face, then she stretched out on the queen-sized bed, pulled the handmade quilt folded at the end over herself, and stared out the window at Flathead Lake, the stars sparkling on the water like diamonds. She'd forgotten how beautiful it was. It had been years since she'd been up here—not since she was a freshman in college. Life got in the way, kept her away. But the last fight with Trace sent her racing across the country to the one place that had always been her home.

She hoped it would be the one place Trace wouldn't find her.

Trace's temper hadn't been an issue when they started dating. Six months into their relationship, he'd begged her to move in with him, and that was when she noticed the change. He was quick to anger, often over the silliest things—losing a life on a video game resulted in the destruction of a game console, something not working the way he expected caused a blow-up of epic proportions, irritation over a missed phone call or an unanswered text caused an over-the-top argument. When she came home later than expected from a night out with the girls, Trace had punched a hole in a wall.

The first time he hit her, it had shocked the shit out of her. Her parents, in particular her father, were tranquil, quiet people. In her twenty-five years on the earth, she had never seen her father lose his temper, not once. Violence and anger were not a part of her life.

It happened less than two months after they moved in together. She'd worked late and failed to call Trace to tell him she was running behind. She stepped in the front door of their shared apartment and called his name, an apology on her lips. She found him leaning against the kitchen counter, his arms crossed, a cold, dead look in his eyes. Serena stopped in front of him and before she could open her mouth to explain, his hand connected with her cheek, whipping her head to the side and making her eyes water.

"That's for being late," he growled. He grabbed her arm, twisted it behind her back, and yanked her close. Serena bit her lip to hold back a cry as her shoulder wrenched and throbbed. Trace grabbed her hair with his other hand, wrapped it around his fingers, and pulled. "Don't do it again. Use your fucking phone." He released her, pushing her away from him.

Serena stumbled over her own feet and fell, her jaw rattling as her teeth clamped down on her tongue. Trace stepped over her and walked away, the bedroom door slamming closed behind him. She burst into tears, shame and guilt overwhelming her.

After a few minutes, she pushed herself to her feet and splashed some cold water on her hot cheeks. She contemplated gathering her things and leaving, but she didn't know where to go. Her parents didn't like Trace; both had told her on separate occasions they had a bad feeling about him. She'd been adamant they were wrong. How was she supposed to go to her parents and tell them he'd hit her? Her sister was at school in Alabama; she couldn't stay with her. She didn't have any close friends; after she and Trace started dating, she'd lost touch with most of them. She had nowhere to go.

Her cheek throbbed, so she grabbed a bag of frozen peas from the freezer and wrapped it in a kitchen towel. She gingerly held it to her cheek and sat on the couch.

Half an hour later, Trace emerged from the bedroom. He pressed a kiss to the top of her head, poured her a glass of her favorite wine, and turned on one of her favorite movies. He sat beside her and wrapped an arm around her waist, his nose brushing against her neck.

"I'm sorry, baby," he murmured. "I was just so worried, and I got all worked up. I lost my temper. It won't happen again—I promise."

Except, it did happen again. And again. And again. Repeatedly over the next eighteen months.

Serena left after Trace nearly killed her. They'd argued over something stupid, and in his anger, he'd shoved her, knocking her into a wall before punching her repeatedly in the kidneys. She'd curled into the fetal position, her arms wrapped around her head, begging him to stop as he pummeled her. The only reason he'd stopped short of beating her to death was because his phone rang, drawing him out of whatever weird, crazy trance he'd fallen into. He'd stopped, spun around, and walked away, leaving her a bleeding, bruised mess on the floor. He disappeared into the bedroom, typical behavior after he abused her. She knew she didn't have a lot of time before he returned.

It occurred to her if she didn't leave Trace, he might kill her. It was sheer luck he hadn't yet. If she didn't leave, she might not live to do it at all. She crawled across the floor, snagged her purse off the table, and texted her father two words.

Daddy, help.

It had taken all her strength to get off the floor and out the front door. She'd dragged herself down the street to the corner store and hid inside to wait for her father, keeping in constant contact with him by text message.

That had been the start of a year of running. Trace did everything in his power to get her back, but she held strong with her parents' help. She moved out of her and Trace's house and out of the city. She got a new job, bought a new car, moved into a new apartment, and tried to start over.

But Trace kept finding her. It didn't matter where she went or what she did, he would show up within weeks of her moving or starting a new job. When her sister, fresh out of college, took a job in Arizona, Serena moved there, too. Another fresh start. After three months, she thought maybe things were getting better. She hadn't heard from Trace or seen him since she'd left California; she believed it was over, for good this time.

She got too comfortable, too complacent.

He'd been waiting for her when she got home from work, sitting in her living room, drunk off his ass. He tackled her as soon as she walked through the door, his hand over her mouth. She bit him and kicked him, somehow by the grace of God connecting with his balls. He released her, allowing her to get away. She locked herself in the bedroom and called 911. The police showed up and arrested Trace, but she knew how it worked; he wouldn't be in jail long. With her sister's help, she'd loaded up her car and left, driving to Flagstaff before calling her father and asking him what she should do. They'd decided Montana was the only place she could go.

———

Serena awoke with a jerk, tumbling from the bed to the floor, a muffled scream clawing its way out of her throat, vestiges of the dream still eating at her psyche.

She pushed herself to her hands and knees as angry, frightened tears fell on the dusty wood floor. She reminded herself nothing could harm her; Trace was not sleeping in the bed beside her, Trace wasn't hiding down the hall or behind the door. She was far away from him. He wouldn't find her. Not here. She took a deep breath, swiped a hand over her damp cheeks, and stood up. She needed coffee.

"Shit," she muttered under her breath as she stared into a bare kitchen cupboard. She opened several others, finding them empty as well. No food in the house. Her parents stocked the house with linens, kept the electricity and the water on, but there was no reason to keep food in a house no one lived in.

The lake house, a condo, was in Lakeside, Montana on Flathead Lake, the largest freshwater lake west of the Mississippi. When she was a kid, her parents bought the condo—an investment according to her father—and every summer growing up, they packed their daughters into the car for the long drive across the country from California to Montana to spend anywhere from two weeks to two months soaking up nature—if nature included a pool, a marina, and an eighteen-hole golf course within walking distance. After Serena and her sister moved out and started their lives, her parents tried to keep up the tradition of visiting every summer, but it had gotten more difficult with every year that passed. It had been ten years since she had been there and at least two since her parents had visited. She hadn't realized they still owned it until her father offered it in a last-ditch effort to keep her safe. Serena agreed, and he'd called ahead to have Clint, the year-round maintenance guy, get the place ready. Apparently, that hadn't included stocking the place with food.

Serena grabbed her phone to search for the nearest grocery store, but before she could, her father's picture popped up on the screen. She forgot she'd promised to call him upon her arrival. He was probably worried sick.

"Hi, Daddy," she answered.

"Goddammit, Serena," Mel Chasey grumbled. "What did I tell you?"

"I know. I'm sorry. I fell asleep after I unloaded the car, and I just woke up. In fact, I was about to look for the nearest grocery store. I need food."

Her father mumbled something under his breath, and she could picture his face—resigned and irritated. "Alright, you're forgiven. How was the drive?"

"Long," she replied. "Exhausting. I'm glad to be here though. Thank you for this. I appreciate it so much."

"I would do anything for you, sweetheart," he murmured. "Anything. All that matters is you're safe."

Fresh tears sprang to her eyes. Serena sometimes forgot how much of a burden the last two years had been on her parents. Swallowing around the lump in her throat, she pushed away the fear threatening to overcome her.

Her father cleared his throat. "You got the credit card I gave you?"

"Yes." It was in her wallet and her only source of income.

"I'm working with the lawyer to get everything moved into new accounts, undetected," he continued. "We'll figure it out. I promise."

"I know you will. Hey, I'm gonna go. I'm starving. I need to get some food. And coffee."

Mel chuckled, then he gave her directions to the nearest grocery store, less than two minutes away. Serena thanked him for the millionth time, said her goodbyes, and grabbed her keys and purse.

A chill shot through her as she stepped outside. Late September in Montana differed from late September in Arizona. It was still in the nineties there, while here, the expected high was in the mid-fifties, and right now it was slightly above forty degrees. The shorts she wore weren't warm enough, but she was desperate for something that wasn't gas station food, so changing clothes would have to wait.

She locked the door behind herself and made her way to the car. As she backed out, she noticed the guy from the condo across the drive walking a beautiful mahogany and black dog in a service vest. She'd never seen a dog quite like him, similar to a German Shepherd, though she didn't think it was. The man was tall, long legged with broad shoulders and thick muscles. He had long chocolate brown hair pulled back in a ponytail, and he'd pushed the sleeves of his sweatshirt up, revealing an intricate tattoo on his left arm. Sunglasses covered his eyes. She waved as she passed him; he ignored her. As she waited for the electric security gate to open, she texted her father.

[Serena: Who's the guy in the condo across from ours? #3, I think?]

She dropped the phone in the cup holder while she drove. It vibrated with an incoming message as she pulled into the grocery store parking lot. She parked and opened the text.

[Dad: His last name is Brooks if I remember correctly. I only talked to him a couple of times. Seemed nice. I believe he's a widow. Moved from NY after his wife's death.]

A widower. And a grouchy one at that. The last thing she needed was another short-tempered jerk in her life. She'd have to do her best to avoid him. She thanked her father for his response, climbed out of the car, and shoved the phone in her back pocket. First thing on her list: coffee. She'd worry about avoiding her new neighbor later.

Chapter Two

Van

Van heard the gate rise before he saw the car. Cars didn't come into the gated community this late, not this time of year. He took his cup of coffee and stepped out on the patio, Soldier at his feet, and leaned on the railing. A woman climbed from the white crossover, the lone streetlight illuminating her. She stretched her arms over her head, her shirt pulling up to reveal her stomach. She turned his direction.

She was tall and curvy, her long caramel-colored hair pulled up in a messy ponytail on the top of her head. A worn pair of shorts and a long-sleeved t-shirt covered her. She was stunning.

He took a step back, startled at the thought bouncing around his head. It had been more than three years since he had found anyone attractive or even looked at another woman with any interest. He'd been too busy hiding from everyone and everything, too busy letting his grief consume him to notice anyone else existed.

He scowled, irritated his thoughts had wandered that direction. He spun on his heel and went back inside.

His phone vibrated from the end table. He snatched it up and hit the button.

"You are the only person who calls me this late," Van growled. "You know that, right?"

"It's because I'm the only person who knows you don't sleep," Lincoln, his best friend, chuckled. "You have a cup of coffee in your hand right now, don't you?"

Van grunted and rolled his eyes. Sometimes, he hated how well Lincoln knew him. He dumped his coffee in the sink and rinsed out the cup. If it wasn't in his hand, he didn't have to lie to Lincoln about it.

"How are you, Van?"

"I'm fine," he grumbled.

"You're a terrible liar." Lincoln sighed. "Seriously, how are you? Are you getting any sleep?"

"A little." Van shrugged, even though Lincoln couldn't see him. "A couple of hours a night, I guess. Better than nothing, right?"

"I guess." Lincoln paused, waiting for his friend to talk. Van kept quiet. "Anything new happening?" he pressed.

"Some woman is at the condo across the drive," he blurted, his mouth getting ahead of his brain. Why the hell had he said that?

"Oh. Um, okay." Lincoln cleared his throat. "You say hi or anything? I mean, you two have to be the only people up there right now."

"Sam and his wife were here last weekend," he muttered.

— *Van* —

"Evan." Lincoln rarely used his full name. It meant Van had irritated him.

"No, I haven't talked to her," Van said. "She *literally* pulled in ten minutes ago." Through the windows along the front of the condo, he could see the woman outside pulling a duffel bag and a suitcase from the car. She looked over her shoulder every few seconds, taking in her surroundings. His curiosity piqued, he watched her as she hurried to take her things inside, her eyes darting around as if she was looking for danger. He saw the nervous, frightened look on her face.

"Nobody's stayed over there in forever," he continued, turning away from the window after the woman armed the car's alarm and went inside. "The owners live in California and haven't come up in a couple of years. I met them once or twice. It looks like she might stay for a while, though."

"Huh," Lincoln mumbled. "You should definitely say hi."

"Maybe. Look, I gotta go. Soldier's sitting by the door staring at me. I gotta take him for a walk before we go to bed."

"Sure. Hey, I thought I'd come up next week. Stay for a few days. I need a break, and I've got a few business things we should discuss."

Van knew what his best friend was doing and why. Every fiber of his being screamed at him to tell Lincoln to stay home, but he could use the company. He *needed* the company. Especially with the three-year anniversary coming up.

"Yeah, I'd like that." He pictured the smile lighting up Lincoln's face. He didn't want to listen to him gloat. "Gotta go." He disconnected the call before his friend said anything else.

He hated to admit it, but he missed Lincoln. They grew up together, joined the Army together, and served in Afghanistan together. They had seen things no man should see and come home still friends. Even though he missed his childhood friend, he couldn't bring himself to move back to New York. Not now, maybe not ever. Too many painful memories. And even though it meant he had to run their security business alone, Lincoln didn't complain or push Van to come home. He did nothing but support him. Van didn't deserve a friend like Lincoln Dunn.

He snatched the leash off the counter and kneeled next to his Belgian Malinois, Soldier. He rubbed the dog's flank, attached the leash to his collar, and pressed a kiss to the top of the dog's head before rising to his feet.

"Let's go, boy," he sighed, opening the door.

She kissed him on the corner, damn the paparazzi, before she laughed and skipped up the street, smiling back at him and waving over her shoulder. Her contagious enthusiasm made him smile. He shouted after her to wait, but she ducked into the coffee shop, her laughter floating back to him, sweet and vibrant over the sound of the busy New York streets.

Van sighed. What was the point of a bodyguard if she wouldn't let him protect her?

The first scream he heard wasn't hers, but it had him shoving the street vendor who'd stopped him out of the way and darting through the crowd, knocking aside the shocked bystanders. He reached her just as Stockwood dropped the match, the gas igniting with a giant whoosh that knocked the air out of him and sent him stumbling backward. He

— Van —

threw himself at her, the fingers of his left hand twisting in her blouse, the flames dancing up his arm—

Van shot out of bed, clutching his left arm, phantom pains burning into the muscle and bone. Startled, Soldier barked, his loud yip stinging Van's ears. He fell to the floor, shoved himself to his feet, hit the wall, and fumbled for the light switch, the breath tearing in and out of his throat, head pounding, eyes burning with unshed tears. He got the light on before he slid to the floor, still clutching his arm.

Soldier jumped off the bed and sat beside him, whining.

"I'm okay, boy," he mumbled. He lifted his arm, allowing Soldier to slip under it and curl up beside him, his head on Van's lap, staring at his master. Hot tears slid down his cheeks and a sob clung to the back of his throat. He gasped for air, his fingers twisting in Soldier's fur. He dropped his head, burying his face against the dog's flank, the sobs breaking free.

Once he could breathe again, he stood up, pulled on some jeans and a Henley from the closet, and grabbed the bottle of scotch from the floor beside the bed. He pushed open the sliding glass door, stepped onto the small balcony, dropped into the lone chaise lounge chair with a heavy sigh, and set the bottle on the floor. He checked his watch, the illuminated dial informing him it was just after three a.m. Two hours of sleep.

He looked out at the lake, the full moon sparkling like a gem on the water. Soldier slipped past the curtain covering the door and walked to Van's side. He absentmindedly patted the dog's head, his thoughts consumed with images from the past. The dog climbed onto the lounge chair and settled himself between Van's legs, his head on his master's stomach.

"Oof." Van grunted as the seventy-plus pound dog climbed on him. "You're not a lapdog, dude."

Soldier gave him a look, and Van swore if dogs could scoff, he would have. Instead, he closed his eyes and fell asleep.

Van relaxed into the chair and scratched between the dog's ears, staring at the surrounding night, sipping from the liquor bottle on the floor. He loved the lake this time of year; it was quiet, and the summer guests had gone home. He was the only year-round resident in the condos, though that hadn't been the plan when he and Adelaide purchased it six years ago. Now and then, some of the other summer residents—those who lived in Missoula or northern Idaho—would come around for a weekend, but no one else was there year-round.

Summers stressed him out. The sleepy town overflowed with vacationers and tourists, strangers mixed in with the familiar faces of the town's residents. He always felt a sense of relief once Labor Day passed, knowing the tourists would leave. The college students were hard to deal with, but he'd gotten good at avoiding them over the years, staying close to home and out of the popular hangouts. It still wasn't as crazy as living in New York.

A light came on in the condo across the way, reminding him of the unexpected visitor. He saw her moving behind the closed blinds, then a few minutes later, the kitchen light came on. The woman who appeared out of nowhere was a curiosity. She seemed skittish and nervous; he was always hypervigilant about those things, noticing the little things others didn't.

His breath caught in his throat, an unwanted memory forcing itself to the surface. He scrubbed a hand over his

— Van —

face. He didn't always notice everything; the one time he should have, the one time it had mattered more than anything, he had failed miserably. A shiver raced through his body, and tears filled his eyes again. He swiped at them, furious with himself. It had been months since he'd had a breakdown, months since he'd let the memories of that day consume him. The approaching anniversary weighed heavily on him.

Van grabbed the bottle and downed the rest of the alcohol inside. God, he'd give anything for a good night's sleep. Surviving on three or four hours—or less—a night for the last three years was slowly destroying him. Two days ago, he'd noticed gray hairs in his beard and several strands in his hair. Wrinkles had appeared on his forehead and at the corners of his eyes. He felt out of sorts, unable to function as he once had, doubting every choice, every decision. He didn't trust himself anymore. Not like he had before Adelaide—

"Nope. Not going there," he grunted, lifting Soldier off his legs and throwing the blanket to the side. He slipped on his shoes, then he whistled for the dog. "Come on, boy. Let's go for a walk."

Chapter Three
Serena

The trip to the grocery store exhausted her. Constantly looking over her shoulder, worrying Trace would appear out of nowhere, messed with her psyche. By the time she filled the cart with all the groceries she thought she might need, a thin layer of clammy sweat covered her, her hands shook, and her heart pounded so hard it hurt. Checking out seemed to take an eternity, the man behind the register chatting about every item she purchased. She nodded politely and smiled, though she was sure it didn't reach her eyes. Once her things were bagged, she mumbled her thanks and rushed out the door.

Back at the condo, Serena backed the car right up to the side door and hurried to unload. After everything was inside, she slammed the door, threw the deadbolt, and slid to the floor, her head in her hands, her breath tearing in and out of her throat. It took a few minutes to get herself under control before she could put everything away.

She'd hoped she could get to the retailer at the edge of town to buy some warm clothes, but after the grocery store, she wasn't sure she could deal with another trip away from the condo. Not right away. Instead, she hauled blankets out of the second bedroom and pulled a few of her favorite movies from the drawer under the television. She made a pot of coffee and a bagel, then she settled in for the day, content to stay inside, hiding away from the world.

Halfway through the second movie she wasn't watching—it was background noise while she drifted in and out of consciousness—she glimpsed the guy from the condo across the way and his dog heading toward the marina. She sat up and watched as they walked down the pier and climbed aboard a beautiful gray speedboat. Within minutes, he was in open waters, headed who knew where, the dog perched on the stern, his mahogany and black fur ruffled by the wind.

Serena sank back into the cushions and closed her eyes. Her curiosity about her neighbor surprised her; after everything she'd been through, men should have been off her list. All men, even handsome, mysterious widowers who lived across the street.

Serena pulled the blanket tighter around herself, shivering as the cool air hit her bare feet. After going to bed at 8 p.m., she woke up around 3:30, forcing herself out of a nightmare, the same one she'd had for months, dreams of Trace chasing her. She stumbled around in the dark and tried to find the light, smashing her toe into the corner of the wall, bringing tears to her eyes.

— *Serena* —

After injuring her foot, there was no sense going back to sleep. Not that she would anyway, not when she couldn't shake off the vestiges of the past or the recurring nightmare.

She should be grateful she had slept at all. Prior to coming to Montana, she'd been lucky to get an hour or two a night. She felt better since her arrival, more at home than she'd been in the last year and a half. Her house in California was the stuff of nightmares and horror movies, more frightening than comforting. The half a dozen apartments she'd lived in after she left California were nothing more than stopping points on the road to freedom, a freedom she could never quite grasp. Arizona had felt like home until Trace had ripped it away from her, forcing her to run. Again.

Here in Lakeside, Serena felt normal. Free. She'd always loved the small college town. It was beautiful, pure, a wonderful place to live. Every summer, she begged her parents to move from their home in California to Lakeside. Over time, she'd forgotten how much she loved the Montana town. It had taken less than forty-eight hours for her to fall in love with Lakeside all over again.

No one from her old life—the one she'd shared with Trace—knew about this place: only her family. They would never tell. Her family craved her freedom almost as much as she did. She prayed this time it worked. She could make a home here, settle down, start over. Maybe she'd go back to school; her degree in marketing wouldn't do her much good here, but maybe she could find a new passion. A fresh start.

Serena pinched the bridge of her nose and sighed, sinking deeper into the couch, deeper into the blankets. She was wide awake, her eyes burning. She wanted to sleep for a week, maybe two. The muscles in the back of her neck and in her shoulder twinged, drawing a weary groan from her. She pushed herself to her feet; she needed to move, to shake off the stiffness the lack of movement caused.

If she were going to live here, she needed to make it her own. Get rid of the old stuff belonging to her parents, bring in some things that belonged to her. She'd start by cleaning, which was cathartic for her. She spent the next couple of hours dusting, wiping down walls, vacuuming, cleaning the bathrooms, and rearranging things, boxing up some old, outdated knick-knacks and even moving the furniture. As she cleared away several years of dust and rearranged things, she realized she was still missing a lot of supplies, along with warm clothes, socks, boots, and a coat.

She was at the store as soon as the sun came up, her cart loaded with long-sleeved t-shirts, sweaters, jeans, socks, a few sweatshirts, a heavy jacket, gloves, and a hat. She picked up a new comforter for the bed and some new sheets, a few candles, some cleaning supplies, and a couple of books she'd been meaning to read. The credit card took a hit, but she knew her father would understand.

By nine, she was back at the condo. She made coffee and breakfast while she watched the news, and the new comforter tumbled around the washing machine. After she put it in the dryer and started the sheets, she grabbed a book and sat on the chair in front of the immense picture window overlooking the lake. Instead of reading, Serena stared at the water lapping gently against the shore.

She tossed the book on the table, tugged on one of her new sweatshirts, and stepped outside. It was a cool cloudless morning, leading her to wonder if it might warm up in the next few hours. She considered going for a walk, but the thought had her gasping for air and gripping the porch rail so tight her knuckles ached. Doing something so normal scared her. Nothing about her life had been normal for years. *Could I go back to the way things were so easily?* It seemed impossible and frightening.

"Fuck it," Serena muttered to herself. "I can do this." She sucked in several deep breaths and stepped off the porch.

She strode across the small lawn and up the road. There was a small bench in the park on the other side of the marina; if she could make it there, she'd be okay. She could do it. Her fear was unnecessary; Trace was over a thousand miles away on the other side of the country. He couldn't hurt her. Once she started down the road by the golf course, she could see the bench. She focused on it and the calm, blue water on the other side of it, repeating to herself she could do it.

When she lowered herself to the bench, a smile playing at the corners of her mouth, it was as if someone had lifted a weight from her shoulders. It had been almost freeing, the walk to the park. For the first time in what felt like forever, she could breathe. She leaned back and closed her eyes, soaking up the morning sun.

Something cold nudged her hand, startling her, and she squeaked in surprise. She opened her eyes to see the gorgeous mahogany dog sitting by her feet, a beat-up tennis ball in his mouth, his tongue somehow hanging out the other side.

"Well, hi there." Serena laughed.

The dog dropped the ball in her lap, tipped his head to one side, and waited expectantly, tail wagging. She picked up the soggy ball and tossed it ten feet away, near the edge of the water. The dog took off like a shot, snatched up the ball on the go, whipped around, and brought it back to her. He dropped it in her lap, then he turned, waiting for her to throw it again. Before she could pick it up, a loud voice boomed behind her.

"Soldier! *Komen*!"

The dog's ears perked up, and his tail wagged faster. He grabbed the ball off Serena's lap and took off at a dead run. She twisted around in time to see him drop the ball at the feet of the guy from the condo across the street. Like the previous day, his hair was in a ponytail, pulled away from his face, and the sleeves of his long-sleeved Henley pushed up, allowing her a brief glimpse of the tattoo on his arm. He crouched in front of the dog and murmured something to him. The dog dropped his head and rested it on the man's knee, his big, brown eyes staring up at him. He ruffled the dog's fur, kissed the top of his head, picked up the ball, and threw it, much harder than Serena had. It soared through the air so fast it whistled.

"Sorry if he was bothering you," he called. "He's overly friendly."

"It's okay," she replied, rising to her feet. "He wasn't bothering me. He's sweet. What kind of dog is he?"

The man smiled and chuckled under his breath, his gray eyes flashing. "Don't tell him he's sweet. He'll get a big head." He cleared his throat and took a step closer. "He's a Belgian Malinois. His name is Soldier. And I'm Van."

"You live across the street." Serena mentally smacked herself; he knew where he lived.

"I do." Van smiled. "And you are?"

"I'm Serena Chasey." She didn't move closer, but neither did Van. They stood a few feet apart, eyes locked, the only sounds the water slapping the shore and Soldier's panting. After about thirty seconds, he cleared his throat again and shifted from foot to foot.

"Are you here long?" he asked.

"I don't know." She shrugged. She honestly *didn't* know. "It's...it's kind of up in the air right now."

Van nodded and crouched beside Soldier, who was staring up at him, the ball in his mouth. He attached the leash in his hand to the dog's collar and rose to his feet. "Well, it was nice to meet you, Serena. I'm sure I'll see you around. After all, I do live across the street."

Serena caught his wink as he spun around and walked away. "Bye," she mumbled, raising her hand in a half-hearted wave.

Heat flooded her cheeks as she stared at Van's retreating form. *When did small talk become so difficult?* She'd be lucky if Van ever gave her the time of day after her abysmal conversation skills. It had been so long since she'd had so much as a casual chat with anyone, male or female, she had forgotten how to act. She pushed a hand through her hair and for the millionth time, cursed Trace's existence. She returned to her seat on the edge of the bench and stared out over the water, wondering when—or if—she would feel normal again.

Chapter Four

Van

By the time Van got back to his condo, he was shaking and sweating. He ran up the stairs, Soldier on his heels, and shoved open the door, slamming it closed behind him and stumbling to the kitchen. He splashed some cold water on his face, but it did nothing to make him feel better, so he grabbed the bottle of Xanax sitting beside the sink, spun off the lid, dumped out two pills, and swallowed them. Not even bothering with a glass, he sucked the water straight from the faucet, then he dragged himself to the couch and sat down, his head in his shaking hands.

Soldier whined, creeping closer, his leash dragging behind him. He rested his paw on Van's leg and whined again.

"I'm okay, boy," he mumbled, resting his hand on the dog's head. "Come here." He patted the sofa beside him.

Soldier didn't hesitate, jumping up on the couch and curling up beside his human. Van slipped off his leash and tossed it on the side table. He rested his head on the back of the couch and closed his eyes, desperately trying to shake the fear clutching his heart.

What was I thinking, talking to that woman? If his damn dog hadn't been the friendliest creature on the planet, he might have gotten out of the park without having to talk to his new neighbor. He wasn't good with people; shit, he wasn't good *for* people. Everyone he got close to got hurt. Keeping to himself was for the best.

As if to prove him wrong, his phone rang, Lincoln's name popping up on the screen. He contemplated not answering it, but if he didn't, Linc would keep calling.

"Yeah?"

"Is that how you greet your best friend?" Lincoln chuckled.

Van grunted something incoherent as he scrubbed a hand over his face.

"What's wrong?" Lincoln asked.

It shouldn't surprise him Lincoln knew something was wrong; he always did. It's what happened when you'd been best friends with someone your entire life; they knew you inside and out.

"I talked to the girl who's staying across the street," he muttered.

"That's a good thing," Lincoln said. "Right?"

"It was until I freaked out," Van grumbled. "The second I walked away from her, I came unglued. Shaking, sweating, trouble breathing. I'm not even sure how I made it back to the house. I popped two Xanax, and now I'm sitting here cursing myself out and hating myself, so guilty I think I might puke."

"Van—"

— *Van* —

"Don't say it, Lincoln. Don't tell me Adelaide would want me to be happy. Don't tell me she'd want me to move on. I can't, not after..." He blew out a shaky breath. "I love her. I'll always love her—"

"You don't have to stop loving her, Evan," Lincoln interrupted. "Nobody is asking you to stop loving her. It's been three years, and it's time for you to live again. Maybe getting to know your new neighbor could be a start?"

Van's mouth snapped shut. He scrubbed a hand over his face and through his hair, pushing it out of his eyes. Lincoln was right.

"I'm gonna be there Friday," Lincoln said after several seconds of silence.

"You don't have to come."

"Already bought my plane ticket, dude. I'll rent a car in Missoula and drive up. Go buy some steaks and take the cover off the grill you bought. I expect dinner when I get there."

"Yes, sir." Van sighed. "I'll see you on Friday."

He disconnected the call and tossed his phone on the table. He toed off his boots and kicked his feet up, stretching out on the couch. Soldier huffed, got to his feet, rearranged himself between his master's legs, rested his head on Van's knee, and fell back to sleep.

He closed his eyes and breathed deeply, concentrating on relaxing, like all those therapy sessions taught him. Not that he'd cared or even tried, but now and then the things he learned came in handy. He focused on the sounds coming through the open door and windows—the waves lapping against the shore and the birds in the trees. He ignored the sound of his neighbor's door slamming closed, refusing to let himself be curious about her.

Van dozed off, the image of Serena smiling and petting Soldier behind his closed eyes.

The steaks, a couple huge potatoes, and a bunch of asparagus sat on the counter while the beer chilled in the cooler on the patio. Lincoln had called after his plane landed, and he'd gotten his rental car. Van expected him in an hour if the weather held.

He finished making up the extra bedroom and straightened up the bathroom, then he went downstairs to start dinner. He enjoyed being busy; it kept him from thinking too much about Adelaide. He'd already ignored calls from his sister, Rebecca, and Lincoln's mom; he knew they meant well, and they wanted to check on him, but he couldn't talk about it. It had been three years since he'd talked about it; nothing had changed.

Once he had the steaks marinating and the potatoes ready to go in the oven, he grabbed a beer and Soldier's leash. He was out the door and halfway down the stairs when a large white SUV rounded the corner. It parked in his driveway and his best friend stepped out.

Soldier took off like a shot, yanking his leash free of Van's hand to dart down the stairs and into Linc's arms. Lincoln stumbled back into the SUV, laughing at the dog's antics. He set him down, the dog's leash wrapped around one hand, his other hand raised in greeting.

"Loser!" Van yelled, trying and failing to keep the smile off his face. It was good to see Lincoln, especially today. His friend had a way of keeping him centered, keeping him

— *Van* —

sane. Whether he wanted to admit it or not, he was glad Lincoln was there.

He met Lincoln at the base of the driveway and let his friend pull him into a one-armed hug.

"It's good to see you." Lincoln grinned.

"As much as I hate to admit it, I'm glad to see you, too." Van laughed. "Thanks for flying across the country to hang out with me."

"How are you?" Lincoln asked.

"Really, Linc?" Van sighed.

His friend shrugged. "You knew I was gonna ask. Might as well get it out of the way."

"Same. I hate this day." Van scrubbed a hand over his face. "I don't want to talk about it." He cleared his throat. "Let me take Soldier for a walk, and then I'll start dinner."

"I'll tell you what," Linc said. "I'll take Soldier for a walk and *you* start dinner. I'm stiff after flying across the country and driving for the last two hours."

"It's because you're getting old," Van joked. "All right. You take my dog for a walk, and I'll get dinner ready. Give me your keys."

Lincoln tossed him the keys, clicking his tongue twice to urge Soldier to follow him as he took off down the road toward the lake. Van watched them go. After Linc rounded the corner, Van grabbed his duffel bag from the SUV, locked it up, and went inside. He fired up the grill and cut up the asparagus while he waited for the grill to heat.

He'd just put the steaks on and the asparagus in the steamer when the door opened, and Lincoln called his name. Van stepped back inside, only to come face to face with his new neighbor.

Van froze, his mouth dropping open. He glanced at Lincoln, who gave him a sheepish grin as he crouched down to take off Soldier's leash.

"Uh... hi, Van..." Serena mumbled. "I... I hope this is okay."

Lincoln bounded to his feet. "I ran into Serena outside, and we got to talking. She's all alone over there, so I invited her for dinner."

Van raised an eyebrow and grunted. He swallowed and nodded. "Sure. It's...it's great. We've got more than enough food." He spun on his heel and hurried out the back door. He grabbed the tongs and flipped the steaks, muttering under his breath.

"Van?"

He forced a smile on his face before turning around.

Serena stood in the doorway, smiling shyly. "Are you sure you're okay with me staying for dinner? I know you weren't expecting me." She pushed a hand through her hair and shrugged. "I understand if you want me to go."

God, I'm a jerk. She was the only other person in the neighborhood aside from Clint, and he was being an asshole. It wouldn't hurt to let her stay for dinner. Besides, it might keep Lincoln from talking about Adelaide.

"I'm sorry," he murmured. "I'm being an ass. I don't want you to go. I was surprised. You're more than welcome to stay. Would you like a beer?"

"I'd love one." She nodded.

Van grabbed a beer from the cooler and handed it to Serena. "Sorry, I was kind of a jerk. I wasn't expecting company."

"Don't let him fool you." Linc chuckled from behind them. "He's a jerk."

— *Van* —

Van shook his head and glared at his friend over Serena's shoulder. Lincoln shrugged and disappeared back inside.

"How do you like your steak?" Van asked.

"Medium rare. If you don't mind?"

"Woman after my own heart." He smiled. "A steak and beer kind of girl."

Serena laughed, raised her beer above her head, and nodded. God, she was beautiful, especially when she smiled. It lit up her entire face and made her eyes sparkle.

He took a drink of his beer. "What brings you to Montana in the off-season?"

A shadow crossed Serena's face, and she swallowed, her throat clicking. She shifted from foot to foot and stared at something over his shoulder.

"A fresh start, I guess. My parents own the condo. When I needed a place to go, they offered it to me. We used to come up here during the summer, but it's been years since I was here. Funny, this place always felt like home, even though I was only here a few weeks a year."

Van nodded. "I get it. There's something soothing about this place. Aside from how gorgeous it is, it just feels right. My wife and I fell in love with it when we visited, and when we found this place, she was ecstatic. She'd never been happier." A lump rose in his throat and his eyes burned. He hadn't meant to bring up Adelaide, especially not today, but talking to Serena was easy. He wanted to talk to her; he wanted to tell her about himself. He took a drink of his beer, wiped his mouth with the back of his hand, and cleared his throat. "I should check the potatoes."

Serena put her hand on his arm. "I'll do it. I might even set the table." She winked at him and squeezed his arm. "Lincoln knows where things are?"

"He does." He pointed in the kitchen's direction. "Don't let him get out of helping you. He's a lazy bastard."

"I heard that," Lincoln yelled from inside.

"I wasn't trying to be quiet!" Van yelled back.

Serena's laughter followed her inside and made Van smile. He could get used to hearing it.

By the time he finished with the steaks, the potatoes and asparagus were done, and the table set. Lincoln had even started a fire, warming the chilly room. Van shucked his sweatshirt, and Serena took off her heavy sweater.

Dinner was a tremendous success. The food was perfect, and the beers were ice cold. To his surprise, Van didn't think about Adelaide once throughout the entire meal. After they cleared the table and put the dishes in the dishwasher, Serena ordered Van to make coffee before she darted out the door, yelling over her shoulder she'd be right back. Ten minutes later, she was back with a plate covered by a towel.

"Dessert." She whipped off the towel to reveal an enormous stack of homemade chocolate chip and sugar cookies.

"You might be the best neighbor ever." Van chuckled.

Serena blushed and scrubbed a hand through her hair, laughing nervously. Lincoln swooped in, assuaging the awkwardness by playing server and taking everyone's coffee order. They got comfortable in the living room, chatting while they sipped coffee and ate cookies.

Lincoln told Serena about his and Van's security business in New York, going into detail about some of their more colorful employees and a few of their eccentric clients. Van sat back and let him talk. It had always been Linc's strongpoint: small talk, engaging conversations, getting people to open up to him. He was good at it.

— *Van* —

Van had no idea how long they sat in front of the fire talking; time seemed suspended, frozen. He couldn't take his eyes off Serena; she enthralled him, watching her, listening to her. There was something under the surface, something hurting her, bothering her. He could sense it, feel it. That was *his* strongpoint, understanding people on an emotional level. It was why he and Linc made such superb partners; Lincoln got them talking and Van got to the heart of the matter. He'd missed it.

"I gotta get some sleep," Lincoln said, rising to his feet, drawing Van from his musings. "My time zones are all out of whack. Serena, it was lovely to meet you. Don't be a stranger. Van could use another friend beside me."

Van scowled. Nothing like telling Serena he only had one friend.

Serena smiled at Lincoln and nodded. "Thanks for inviting me, Linc. This was… it was nice. I've had a great time." She stood up, too. "I guess I should head home, too."

"I'll walk you." Van shot to his feet before Lincoln could volunteer.

"You don't have to. It's across the street…"

"It's dark, though. I don't want you to walk alone." He grabbed his sweatshirt and held Serena's sweater out to her. "It's not a bother. I promise."

Lincoln stopped halfway up the stairs and ducked his head to look at them. "There's no sense in arguing with him. He's chivalrous to a fault. Let him walk you home."

Serena grinned. "I won't argue." She took the sweater from Van, waved goodbye to Lincoln, and let Van lead her out the door.

Van may have been chivalrous, but walking Serena to her condo was a little foolish. It was across the street, and it took them less than two minutes to get down the stairs and across the road to her door. The light on the porch wasn't on, so the only illumination came from the streetlight on the corner. It cast a dim glow over her front door. They stood in the pale-yellow light, staring at each other like they had the first time they met.

She tucked a strand of hair behind her ear and cleared her throat. "Thanks again for letting me stay for dinner. I'm sorry if Lincoln overstepped his bounds by inviting me."

"Linc frequently oversteps his bounds." Van chuckled. "Especially when it comes to my life."

Serena shook her head and grabbed the doorknob. "He worries about you. At least, that's what he told me."

"He does." He smiled. "I love him for it."

"He's a good friend."

"He is. A better friend than anyone can understand."

Silence fell over them again. Serena scraped her shoe in the dirt next to the doorstep while Van desperately tried to think of something to say. Serena beat him to it.

She pushed open the front door. "Thank you for walking me home."

"You really should lock your door," Van scolded. "Crazy things happen, even in a small town like this."

A funny look crossed Serena's face and her eyes darted around. "I... I didn't think about it. You're right of course." She pivoted to look behind her, her elbow bumping his arm when she turned, her foot coming down on his, causing her to stumble into him. Van grabbed her elbow and the doorjamb to keep them both upright, pulling her against his chest at the same time. The top of her head hit his chin, knocking his head back. He grunted as pain shot through his jaw.

— *Van* —

Serena's hands landed on his chest. "Oh God! Van, I'm so sorry."

"It's okay," he muttered, rubbing his chin. "Trust me: I've had worse." He squeezed her arm. "Are you okay? I didn't mean to scare you."

"I'm fine." She smiled, though it didn't reach her eyes. "Being in a new place makes me nervous, I guess." She moved backward, pulling herself free of his grip as she stepped through the door. "I'll talk to you later." The door closed in his face.

Van exhaled and pushed a hand through his hair. He must have said something to upset her. He didn't know what or how, but he'd done something; otherwise, she wouldn't have reacted that way. A hard knot sat deep in the pit of his stomach. Things had been going so well; he'd had fun for the first time in forever, and he hadn't thought about Adelaide or the fact it was the anniversary of her death even once. *How do I always fuck things up?*

He stared at the closed door, wishing he could think of something to say or do to fix whatever he'd broken. For the first time in three years, he felt alive, like he could breathe. A slamming door had knocked that right out of him. He spun around and stalked back across the street. He didn't know why he'd even tried. He wasn't good for anybody; the world would be better off if he kept to himself.

Chapter Five
Serena

She shut the door in Van's face and sank to the floor, her back against the door, her knees pulled up to her chest. She wanted to stay outside and talk to Van, maybe invite him in for a few minutes, but sudden fear gripped her heart. She needed to get inside where it was safe, away from the oppressing darkness of the night and the possibility of Trace appearing.

Serena wrapped her arms around her head and prayed, prayed for respite from Trace's insane hold over her. She'd hoped the opposite side of the country would be far enough away from the asshole to end it forever.

She pushed herself to her feet and peered out the window, watching Van cross the street, his shoulders stiff. She should open the door and call after him, but the fear wouldn't let her go. Instead, she threw the lock and wandered deeper into the house.

She'd had a good time, a great time. Lincoln was funny and easygoing, while Van was more intense and serious. She could see how they made excellent business partners; they offset each other well. She was insanely curious why Van was in Montana and Lincoln was in New York when they had a business to run. It had to be because of Van's wife. Her father said he was a widower and the things Lincoln told her confirmed it. But what happened?

The more important question was why she was so interested. It wasn't like she was looking for a new man. She didn't want or need a man in her life, not after the way the last one treated her. She should swear off men forever.

So, why can't I stop thinking about my neighbor?

Her interview for the receptionist position was at eleven in the president's office. She'd once been a marketing executive at a high-end advertising firm in Beverly Hills, but she wouldn't find a job like that in Lakeside. She'd applied for several positions at Lakeside University, including the receptionist to the university president. She hadn't expected to interview for it, not when she had zero experience, so getting the opportunity was a blessing. There wasn't a lot to choose from in a town this small—it was the college or nothing, especially during the tourist off-season.

Every time she thought about the upcoming job interview, her stomach churned, and her hands shook. No matter how many times she interviewed for a job, it rattled her. She tossed and turned for hours, drifting in and out of sleep until she finally gave up and got out of bed well before the sun. Wrapped in a heavy sweater, she sat on the patio with her coffee, watching the sun sparkle on the lake as it rose behind her. A breeze came in off the water, making her shiver.

Voices rose in the air behind her; two men laughing and the playful yipping of a dog. Van and Lincoln. They walked past her condo, headed down the road toward the marina. She considered calling after them, but she bit her tongue and watched them walk by.

Two gorgeous men: one broken and the other longing to help him heal. When she'd run into Lincoln on Friday, and he'd invited her to dinner, he had warned her Van might not love the idea of her being there, even explained why. She'd tried to beg off, but he was insistent, persuasive, reminding her she should get to know her neighbor. He'd promised to be a buffer, but it hadn't been necessary. Van had been wonderful.

They got on the same boat she'd seen Van get on last week. A few minutes later, they headed for the middle of the lake, Soldier sitting on the stern, an adorable doggie grin on his face. Serena wished she were with them, though she didn't want to insert herself in their friendship. She was a neighbor who barely knew either of them.

It wasn't like she had time for fun anyway. The job interview was less than two hours away. Getting a job was at the top of her to-do list. She couldn't keep relying on her father for money; it didn't feel right.

She needed more coffee. Lack of sleep made caffeine a priority. She stood up and watched Van's boat speeding across the water for a few minutes before she went inside. Nervous energy kept her moving; she straightened up the living room, washed the few dishes in the sink and put them away, then she made another cup of coffee.

Despite her exhaustion, she felt energized and ready to conquer the day, if not the world. A shower helped wake her up, and the familiar routine of getting ready calmed her nerves. She went easy on the makeup—she didn't have much anyway—then she dried her hair until it cascaded over her shoulders and framed her face. She pulled on a pair of dark gray cords and a blue sweater, shoved her feet into her favorite boots, and switched the few paltry items in her backpack to her purse. A last glance in the mirror on her way out gave her a boost in confidence. For once, she didn't look or feel like she was on death row.

Maybe things were going to take a turn in a good direction.

Charles Ross shook his head and chuckled. "You're seriously over-qualified, Ms. Chasey. You have a bachelor's degree in marketing, and you're applying for a position as an administrative assistant. I feel guilty even *suggesting* you take the job."

"Are you offering it to me?" Serena smiled.

"Yes," Charles replied. "But are you sure this is what you want? There must be something better out there for you. Maybe in Missoula?"

"I live here in Lakeside, Mr. Ross. I want to work here."

"Then the job is yours," Charles said. He rose to his feet and held his hand out. "Can you start next week?"

"I could start tomorrow." She laughed, shaking the university president's offered hand.

"Well, I think my current assistant might take offense to getting kicked out a week early." He grinned. "I look forward to seeing you next week, though. Stop and see Marcie on your way out. She'll give you your paperwork and tell you where to return it."

"Thank you so much, Mr. Ross," Serena gushed. "I can't tell you how much I appreciate this." She prayed he didn't notice the tears gathered at the corner of her eyes. She would cry once she was in her car.

"Call me Charlie." He shook her hand. "I'll see you soon."

Serena floated out the door, her feet inches off the ground. Marcie was extremely helpful, even putting her cell phone number at the top of the employee handbook so Serena could contact her with questions. Marcie invited her to come in on Friday for a few hours so she could acclimate herself with the office and ask questions. Serena readily agreed.

On her way home, she decided she should celebrate. She stopped at the store and grabbed a couple bottles of wine and a sour cream cake with a brown sugar glaze. She also picked up a rotisserie chicken, a salad, and some vegetables. It was too much food for one person, but at least she'd have leftovers for a few days.

Back at the condo, she noticed Lincoln's rental wasn't in the driveway anymore. Maybe he and Van had gone out for burgers at the country club or something. If she remembered correctly, they had exceptional burgers.

Serena parked next to her condo and stepped out of the car. Van came around the corner, Soldier walking beside him, off his leash. As soon as the dog saw Serena, he darted up the road and slid to a stop in front of her. He bumped his head against her leg, pushing her against her car.

"Hey there, buddy," she murmured, crouching beside him.

"Wow, he is really taken with you." Van laughed. "I'm sorry he keeps bugging you."

"He's no bother at all." Serena scratched Soldier behind the ears, earning herself a sloppy kiss on her cheek. "He's sweet." She bounded to her feet. "I thought maybe you and Lincoln went to grab a burger or something."

Van shook his head. "Linc is on his way to Missoula. He has a 5 a.m. flight back to New York."

"Oh," she mumbled. "He, uh, didn't stay long."

Van shrugged. "Gotta get back to business." He glanced in the back seat of her car and cleared his throat. "Can I help you take your groceries in?"

"Sure." She nodded. She pulled open the door and let Van take the bags out while she unlocked the door. He followed her inside, Soldier at his heels, and set the bags on the kitchen counter. He nodded at her and turned to leave.

"Would you like to stay for dinner?" she blurted.

"I wouldn't want to impose."

"No imposition. I promise. I'd love some company. It's no fun celebrating by yourself."

"Celebrating?" Van inquired, his head tipped to the side, one eyebrow raised. "What are you celebrating?"

"I got a job today." She grinned, bouncing on her toes. "The administrative assistant to Lakeside University's president."

"That's outstanding! Congratulations!" A smile lit up Van's face, and Serena couldn't help but think how gorgeous he looked.

"So, will you stay? I have chicken, vegetables, and a salad, plus two bottles of wine. I have more than enough to share."

"I'll stay." Van nodded. "Let me run Soldier home—"

"No." She interrupted. "He can stay. He'll behave himself, right?" She shot a playful, stern look in Soldier's direction. He barked in response, which made her laugh.

"He better." Van chuckled. "At least let me help."

Serena smiled. "You can clean and chop the vegetables while I change. The cutting board is in the cupboard, and the knives are in the top drawer." She left Van to work and went to change her clothes.

She slipped on a pair of jeans, a long-sleeved t-shirt, and a pair of fuzzy socks, then she pulled her hair into a low ponytail. By the time she got back to the kitchen, the salad was made, the vegetables cut, sprinkled with olive oil, and in the oven. Van had also poured two glasses of wine, set them on the table, and was poking around her fireplace.

"This is a mess," he stated. "I'll call Clint—ask him to come by and clean it. Don't use it until he does; it's a fire hazard."

"Okay." She nodded. "Thanks. I probably would have tried to start a fire and burned the place down." She handed him a glass and sat on the edge of the couch. She took a sip of the crisp white wine and sighed.

"Tell me about your new job," Van urged, sitting on the opposite end of the couch.

Serena launched into a brief explanation of her new position, which somehow turned into a discussion about how nervous she'd been and how badly she needed the job. Van listened intently, his gray eyes locked on hers. When she stopped talking, he was nodding.

"It's hard to start over." For the first time since they'd sat down, he didn't look at her, his gaze drifting to the large picture window facing the lake. "You think you can't do it, and every day you struggle to get through the day without losing it. It seems like it goes on forever until one day you wake up, and it's a little easier to make it through, and the next day is easier, and the next even easier. Of course, then you feel guilty because it's getting easier, which makes you wonder if you're forgetting what was once important in your life." He rubbed his hand over his left arm, and Serena could have sworn there were tears in his eyes.

"Van–" she began.

"Nothing's harder than starting over when you don't want to, though. When your entire world turns upside down and everything changes and you *have* to change, even when it kills you inside. Starting over after losing the person you loved more than anything in the world is the worst."

The timer on the stove went off, and Van shot to his feet, swiping at his eyes as he brushed past her to take the vegetables from the oven. She followed him into the kitchen, and together they dished up the food and refilled their wine glasses. They sat at the breakfast bar, the silence between them thick and uncomfortable. Serena shifted in her seat and stabbed her fork into her vegetables. She glanced at Van, who looked as uncomfortable as she felt. She took another sip of wine and decided to hell with it.

"Van? Can I ask what happened to your wife?" she asked. She knew he probably wouldn't want to answer, but she had to try.

Van laid his fork beside his plate and wiped his mouth with his napkin. He wouldn't meet her eyes. "I don't like to talk about what happened."

"I'm sorry. I understand if it's too difficult to talk about. Forget I asked."

Serena endured a few more minutes of uncomfortable quiet, nothing to fill the emptiness but the scrape of silverware across the plates and Soldier's snorts and yips as he dreamed. Just when she thought she couldn't endure another minute of the suffocating silence, Van cleared his throat.

"My wife was Adelaide Brooks."

"The actress?" Serena asked. "I love her movies. She was wonderful."

Van nodded. "She was amazing. Even though most of her work was in California or Canada, we lived in New York because it was home for both of us. She'd gotten popular enough I thought she should have security; she hated the idea. I won. Lincoln assigned one of our best men to head up the detail. Jasper traveled with her when I couldn't, kept an eye on her when I wasn't able to. I trusted him with her life." He picked up his wine and downed what was left in the glass, then he grabbed the bottle and filled the glass to the brim. "Six months after we assigned him to Adelaide, she went to Lincoln and begged him to take Jasper off her detail. After a lot of coaxing, she admitted he'd hit on her, rather aggressively. She didn't want to tell me. She told Linc she was afraid I would do something stupid."

"Did you?"

Van shook his head. "No. I did fire him. He was furious, claimed he and Adelaide were in love and she was lying to save my feelings. I didn't believe him; Adelaide would never do that to me. We'd been in love since high school; we were inseparable. I took over her security detail. For months we dealt with Jasper stalking Adelaide: phone calls, emails, showing up at movie premieres, on the set of a television show she was shooting, even at our apartment in New York. The only peace we got was a two-week vacation here. Once we were back home, it started all over. We got a restraining order. I took the security detail down to a bare minimum to keep her whereabouts a secret; I did everything to keep her safe. He terrified her. Absolutely terrified her."

"What happened?"

"Adelaide had gotten a part in a Broadway show, so we were in New York. She convinced me to take her to her favorite coffee shop, said she was tired of being cooped up at home, hiding from the world. I agreed. She was a bright light, so full of life and energy—the opposite of me. I couldn't resist giving her what she wanted." Van rubbed a hand over his face and exhaled. Tears glistened on his cheeks. "Sorry. I... I haven't talked about this in a long time."

Serena rested her hand on his arm and smiled gently. "It's okay. Take your time."

Van cleared his throat and took another drink of wine. "I got hung up outside talking to some street vendor, let her out of my sight for a minute. It was too long. I heard her scream... and... and..." He brushed at the tears streaming down his face, his voice dropping to a low whisper. "By the time I got to her, Jasper had covered her in gasoline and was standing beside her. He lit a match and dropped it, engulfing them both in flames. I threw myself at Adelaide, tried to grab her but... it... it was useless."

Van shoved up the sleeve of his shirt on his left arm, revealing the intricate tattoo she'd glimpsed several times. Loops and swirls covered his arms from the wrist to the elbow. Beautiful artwork hid the deep scars burned into his skin. Serena ran a finger over the markings, a tear sliding down her own cheek.

"I'm so sorry." The pain he must have suffered; she couldn't fathom what he'd gone through.

Van tried to smile, but it came across as a painful grimace. "After her funeral, I moved here. I can't go home."

"This is your home now," Serena said. "I'm sure Adelaide would be happy to know you've made a home here. You said she loved it."

"She did."

"Well, she'd want you to be happy."

Van chuckled. "That's what Lincoln always says."

"He's a smart man." Serena laughed. She squeezed his arm and decided it was time to change the subject. "Hey, how about we have some dessert and some more wine?"

"I think I'll take a raincheck," Van replied, pushing himself to his feet. "I should get home." He snapped his fingers to get Soldier's attention. "Soldier, *komen*." The dog jumped to his feet and went to his master's side. "Thanks for dinner."

Serena could only watch, speechless, as he left, closing the door quietly behind himself.

Chapter Six
Van

Van took Soldier for his morning walk before the sun was up, then he holed up in the house for the rest of the day, hiding from Serena. He told himself it was for the best; he wasn't the kind of person a woman like Serena needed in her life. She didn't need a trainwreck like him invading her space. As much as he was drawn to her, he knew staying away would be better for her.

The knock on the door came when he was heating a can of soup for dinner. He contemplated not answering it, but the knock came again, louder and more insistent. He turned off the stove and went to the door, Soldier at his feet.

"I know you're in there, Van," Serena yelled. "You might as well open the door."

Soldier barked, earning himself a dirty look from his owner. Van pushed a hand through his hair, gathered it at the back of his neck, and wrapped the rubber band from his wrist around it. Then he yanked the door open.

"Hey," he said. "What's up?"

"I know you're avoiding me," Serena said. "I think I even understand why."

"Serena—"

"Let me finish," she snapped. "I understand better than you can imagine. But right now, I think we could both use a friend. I like you; you're a good guy. And I think you like me—at least I hope you do. I guess all I'm asking is if we can be friends. Trust me, Van. That's all I want. A friend."

Van held the door open and gestured for her to come in. She snatched a paper bag off the ground by her feet and stepped inside.

"Chicken sandwiches," she explained. "And cake, since you bailed on me last night."

"Did you bring the wine?"

"I did. So I can stay?"

"I'm making soup. It'll go great with the sandwiches. You pour the wine, and we'll sit by the fire. It's warmer over there."

"Sounds great." She smiled.

Three weeks after Serena started her new job, she showed up at Van's door and asked him to take her to dinner.

"I need a night out," she explained. "My job is going great, I like the people I work with, and I think it's about time I get to know the town. People keep asking me if I've been to this place or that place, and I have to say no. And

— Van —

it's been forever since I've gone out and had fun. It's Friday, and I don't work tomorrow. I thought I'd let you take me to dinner."

"You'll *let* me take you to dinner? I don't get a choice?"

Serena's jaw moved and her eyes narrowed. A grin spread across her face when she realized Van was teasing her. "Come on, Van. Take me to dinner. It'll be fun. Please?"

Van shook his head and laughed. "Okay, but there's only one place I'll go."

"I'm at your mercy." She shrugged. "Give me an hour?"

"See you then," Van replied.

He hadn't realized he needed another friend until Serena came along. She was exactly what he needed, especially with Lincoln on the other side of the country. She demanded nothing from him, nothing more than his friendship, and it thrilled him.

They'd fallen into an easy, predictable pattern; dinner once or twice a week—sometimes at his place, sometimes at hers—walks with Soldier and breakfast on Saturday or Sunday morning.

Even though they were becoming friends—good friends—Serena held back a part of herself. She didn't talk much about her life before Montana. He didn't know what she'd done, where she'd lived, or even if she'd been involved with someone. No matter how much he pushed, or questioned, or hinted she could confide in him, she wouldn't budge. She was tight-lipped about her life before Lakeside.

He longed to get her to talk to him, like he'd done with her. Telling Serena about Adelaide—something he'd only spoken to Lincoln about—seemed to break down some emotional barrier that had been holding him back. For the first time in three years, he felt alive. He looked forward to getting up in the morning, and he looked forward to seeing Serena, spending time with her, talking to her. He hadn't felt like this in years, not since Adelaide.

Serena was back in one hour. His heart stopped when he opened the door and saw her. She wore a pair of black jeans, a cream sweater, and a red scarf. She had on a pair of high-heeled black boots, bringing her almost eye-level with him. Her long, caramel-colored hair was down, loose curls framing her face. She was gorgeous.

"You're staring," she murmured, blushing.

He chuckled. "Sorry. You clean up nice."

"As do you," Serena observed, eyeing him up and down.

He'd changed into clean jeans, a lightweight gray sweater, and a black leather jacket. He didn't dress up much; this was as close as he got. It pleased him to know Serena approved.

She looped her arm through his. "You driving?"

"Yes, ma'am." He pulled the door closed, then he led her to his truck parked at the back of the condo. He opened the door for her, took her elbow, and helped her inside.

"Where are we going?" she asked.

Van started the truck, backed out of the driveway, and waited for the security gate to open. "My favorite place to eat in this town is the Time Out Bar and Grill. It's close to the college on the water. It has a fabulous view. I think you'll like it."

"Sounds great." She stared out the window for a few minutes. "I can't tell you how much I appreciate this, Van. How much I appreciate you. Things haven't been normal for me in a long time. I've had a few tough years. Extremely tough. Being around you, being your friend, it... it means the world to me. Thank you."

— *Van* —

Out of the corner of his eye, Van saw Serena wiping her eyes with a tissue from her purse. He bit his tongue; it was obvious someone had hurt her. Someone Van now wanted to hurt. He didn't speak, but instead reached across the seat and took her hand, his fingers intertwined with hers.

They drove in silence to the restaurant, but it wasn't awkward or uncomfortable. It was two friends leaning on each other, taking strength from each other. Van suspected his feelings for Serena were becoming more than friendly, morphing into something more. While the thought terrified him, kept him awake at night, he was doing his best to accept it.

Fear kept him from embracing those feelings, fear of the unknown, fear the feelings weren't returned, and fear of being disloyal to Adelaide. His wife had been the first and only woman he had ever loved and feeling something akin to that with another woman felt like a betrayal.

The Time Out Bar and Grill was busy. The parking lot was crowded with cars, and raised voices and loud music spilled out the open door. Serena took Van's hand and leaned into him as they walked to the door. It felt right, her hand in his. He liked it.

It seemed as if everybody was on the dance floor or shoved up against the bar. They weaved through the crowd to the tables at the back of the bar. Serena had a death grip on his hand, squeezing it so tight it hurt. He found a table as far from the crowds as they could get, pulled out Serena's chair for her, and eased into the one beside her.

Her hands shook, and her eyes darted around as if she were looking for danger. She exhaled a shaky breath.

Van slid his chair close to hers and rested his arm on the back of it. "Serena? What is it?"

She shook her head, her lip caught between her teeth, her eyes wide and terrified. "I... I just... I'm sorry, Van. I don't know if I can do this. There are so many people."

He rested his hand in the middle of her back and rubbed gentle circles on it. "Look at me, Serena. I won't let anything happen to you. I promise. But you have to tell me what's wrong."

She turned to face him, fear written in every worry line on her face. "You'll think I'm being stupid," she whispered.

"I won't. Tell me what's wrong."

She dragged in a deep breath, then another before she spoke.

"His name is Trace."

Serena excused herself to splash some water on her face, glancing over her shoulder at least twice on her way to the restroom. While she was gone, their server, Trista, took their order, beers and burgers, promising to get it to them as quick as possible, despite the crowds. Van thanked her. Serena returned a minute later.

"Okay, I'm listening," he said as she eased into the seat.

"Are you sure you want to hear this?" She pushed a shaking hand through her dark curls.

"Yes, I'm sure. As long as you're willing to tell me."

"Trace is my boyfriend... *was* my boyfriend. We were together for a little over a year. I've been hiding from him for almost two. Or trying to hide from him."

The hairs on Van's arms stood up, and a thick knot settled in his gut. "Why are you hiding from him?"

— *Van* —

Serena stared at him, tears glistening in her azure blue eyes. She shrugged. "He hit me, Van. A lot."

Van closed his eyes and gritted his teeth. "He hit you."

"I made him angry—"

"No," he interrupted. "Do not blame yourself for what that piece of shit did."

Serena nodded, the tears now sliding down her cheeks. "I'm sorry."

"Don't apologize. You get to feel whatever you want." He sighed. "So, you came to Montana to get away from this Trace guy. He doesn't know about the condo?"

She shook her head. "No. I never talked about it. My dad thought it would be a good place to get away. To start over. I... I hope he's right. But I still get scared, you know? I've spent two years looking over my shoulder wondering if he was there. I don't feel safe anywhere. Crowds... a lot of people... they scare me. I worry Trace is hiding in the crowd. Who am I kidding? Everything scares me. I desperately want it to be over, I want things to be normal, I want to *feel* normal, but I'm afraid I never will."

Van took her hand and held it between his. "You don't have to be afraid. I will keep you safe. I won't let anything happen to you." The words tasted bitter on his tongue; he'd said the same thing to Adelaide.

"Promise?" Serena whispered.

"I promise."

"All right. Here we go." Trista set their beers and food on the table in front of them, interrupting their discussion. "Can I get you anything else?"

"No, Tris, thank you."

"Who's your friend?" she asked.

Serena smiled at their waitress. "I'm Serena. I'm new here. Van tells me you guys have the best food in town."

"Nice to meet you, Serena. I'm Trista. You can call me Tris." She wiped her hands on her towel then shook Serena's. "The reason Evan thinks we have the best food in town is because we're the only restaurant he'll eat at. But the service is always friendly, and the beer is cold." She patted Van on the shoulder. "Let me know if you need anything else."

"Evan?" Serena said, turning to look at him after Trista left.

Van chuckled. "Full disclosure: my first name is Evan. My nickname is Van."

"I can't believe I've known you for a full month, and I'm just finding out your actual name is Evan. Wow. You think you know people." She shook her head and took a bite of her burger. "Mm, these burgers are good, though."

"You okay?" he asked.

Serena nodded and gave him a half-hearted smile. Van took a drink of his beer and watched her. She tried to act like she was okay, but he could see the fear in her eyes, hear the tremor in her voice when she spoke. His blood boiled; if he ever got his hands on this Trace guy, he would teach him what it felt like to get the shit kicked out of him. Men like Trace were cowards and didn't deserve to have *any* woman in their lives, let alone a woman as good as Serena.

"You're not eating," she mumbled around the food in her mouth. "Not hungry?"

"Yeah, sorry. Off in thought." He grabbed the ketchup and drowned his fries in it, then he dug into his burger.

He let it go, even though he was curious about Trace. He wanted Serena to have a good time tonight. It hadn't

— *Van* —

escaped his notice when she said it had been a long time since things had been normal for her, and not only did it make him angry, it made him determined to give her some sense of normalcy. Trace may have destroyed her, but Van would fix her. It started tonight: excellent food, good beer, and good music. Anything to put a smile on her face.

Starting tomorrow, he would find out everything he could about Trace. And he would make sure the man never hurt Serena again. He would protect her, no matter what.

Chapter Seven

Serena

Serena leaned against Van as he unlocked her door and helped her inside. He flipped the light on in the kitchen and led her to the living room.

Her head spun, and her cheeks felt hot. She'd had too much to drink, but she'd had *fun*. For the first time in years. The food had been fantastic, the music had been loud, and the drinks had flowed. She'd beaten Van at pool, though she suspected he had let her win. Not that it mattered—they were having a good time. Van even smiled a few times. When they played darts, she switched to margaritas, swearing it would improve her aim. All it did was make her giggle and hit the wall beside the dartboard instead of the actual board. She didn't care; she had a great time.

Once Van released her, she leaned over to take off her boots, but all the blood rushed to her head, and she fell forward. Luckily, she landed on the couch, a hiccuping giggle leaving her. She flopped over, yanked her sweater off, leaving her in a light t-shirt, then she stretched out on her back, and stared at the ceiling.

"I need help, Evan." She laughed, kicking her feet.

"I'm gonna kill Trista for telling you my real name," he grumbled. He perched beside her on the couch and pulled her legs into his lap.

It took some maneuvering, but he got her boots off. He got up and set them beside the door, then he grabbed a blanket from the basket at the end of the couch and threw it over her. He crouched beside her and brushed her hair away from her face.

"Get some sleep. When you wake up, drink some water, and take a couple pain pills. I think I saw a bottle of ibuprofen in the kitchen. Otherwise, you'll have one hell of a hangover."

Serena nodded, wincing when it made the room spin. Van patted her arm and stood to leave, but she caught his hand, stopping him.

"Van, wait," she murmured.

"Hm?" he grunted, dropping to his knees beside her.

"Thank you."

"You already said thank you, sweetheart." He laughed. "Several times."

Serena shook her head. "Not for tonight. For everything, listening to me, understanding what I'm going through, and for promising to protect me. It's the first time I've felt safe in over three years. I can't possibly repay you for that."

"You don't have to repay a thing." Van sighed. He brushed a finger down her cheek. "I have to keep you safe; you mean too much to me to let anything happen to you."

— *Serena* —

A gasp escaped her, the air pushed from her lungs as Van's eyes locked on hers. His fingers drifted down her cheek to slide around the back of her neck. Sandalwood and spice washed over her, making her stomach flutter with unexpected need. Serena surged up, her mouth on Van's, the kiss intense, lingering. Her toes curled, her fingers twisted in the lapels of his jacket, her tongue darting out to trace his lower lip.

He abruptly released her. "I have to go," he said.

"You could stay."

Van kissed the corner of her mouth and pushed himself to his feet. "God, Serena, you tempt the shit out of me. But it's been a crazy, emotional night for both of us, and we've both been drinking. I don't think either of us is thinking rationally right now. So, I'm gonna go home. I'll see you in the morning. I'll bring coffee and bagels." He kissed her forehead and then he was gone, the door slamming closed behind him.

Serena shoved the blankets off and swung her legs over the side of the bed. Her stomach rumbled, either from too much liquor or the need to eat. She ran her hands through her hair, pulling it off her neck into a ponytail. She stared out the window at the winter storm rolling across the lake. The clouds touched the water, the wind blew in tremendous gusts, and snow swirled through the air.

She pulled on a pair of jeans, a sweater, boots, and her heavy coat, then she slipped out the door, intent on walking to clear her head. She hadn't slept a wink, not after the kiss, not after Van's revelation.

He cared about her.

At least, she thought it was what he meant when he said she meant too much to him to let anything happen to her. As much as it scared her, she felt the same thing for him. So much had happened in both of their lives—so much pain, so much hurt. Her heart ached for him, for herself, for everything the two of them had gone through, for everything that had broken them. Two broken people drawn to each other. She didn't know if they could make it work. *Why can't things be simple?*

The wind stung her cheeks, sharp needles of cold stabbing into her cheeks. She wrapped her arms around herself, climbed the hill, turned left at the gate, and started down the road next to the golf course.

She walked until she stood on the playground at the park near the water, staring at the lake and the dock, reliving every minute of the previous night. For the first time since everything with Trace, she felt alive. Van brought something to life inside of her, something Trace destroyed while they'd been together. She wanted to grab onto it and never let it go. She wanted Van.

After he'd left last night, she'd chastised herself repeatedly, wondering if she'd pressed him too hard, pushed him too far. Except she knew if she could go back and do it again, she would still kiss Van. And she wouldn't let him leave.

The dock went a hundred feet out into the lake, a wooden bridge floating on the water, secured by a few thin ropes tied to cement poles anchored in the lake. On the windiest of days, the dock swayed side to side; walking on it felt like walking a tightrope suspended over the Grand Canyon. She remembered chasing her sister up and down the dock, laughing, making a game of not falling in the water.

The wind blew through the trees, and the waves crashed against the shore, making the dock rock and sway like a crazy carnival ride. She shivered, zipped her jacket up to her chin, and chided herself for not grabbing her hat and gloves on the way out the door. She hadn't been thinking when she'd left; she had to move, to burn off some of this energy keeping her awake. Ever since she was a kid, she would take a walk when she needed to clear her head, so that had been the first thing she'd thought to do when she woke up for the hundredth time.

Serena followed the path from the playground to the dock and without hesitating, she stepped onto it. Van's anguish over the loss of his wife played like an incessant drumbeat in the center of her chest, ripping her heart to shreds with every tear she remembered falling from his eyes. She wanted to comfort him, to take away the pain she knew he lived with every day, but fear held her back. She wasn't good enough for him; she was too broken.

The stinging bite of the wind against her face drew her from her thoughts. She was steps away from the end of the dock. A strong gust of wind pushed her forward, forcing her to her knees. She stared into the murky depths of the churning waters of Flathead Lake. She hadn't realized she'd walked all the way to the end of the dock. A spray of icy cold water hit her in the face, and another gust of wind made the dock rock dangerously beneath her. Her fingers dug into the wood and splinters embedded themselves in the tips of her fingers. She dragged in a shaky breath and squeezed her eyes closed.

"Serena! What the hell are you doing?"

Fright propelled her forward, the sharp voice startling her, fear gripping her heart and sending her over the edge of the dock and into the freezing water. Her heavy coat sucked up the water like a sponge, and she immediately sank. She flailed her arms—she'd never been much of a swimmer—and tried to scream, but she swallowed the icy water, instantly freezing her throat and making her sputter.

"Serena!"

She heard someone call her name as a wave washed over her, pulling her under. She kicked her feet and reached for the surface, but there was nothing to grab onto. Another wave hit, more water went down her throat, her gasps and cries drowned out by the crashing waves.

Serena struggled to keep her head above water, feet kicking, arms pumping, anything to stay afloat. When she came to the surface again, she glimpsed Van racing toward her, then Soldier launched himself into the water, landing beside her and sending more water over her head. Instinct had her reaching for him, her fingers twisting in his coat, and he was beside her, his breathing loud in her ear as he turned to swim toward the dock with her arms wrapped around his neck.

Van laid down on the dock, his arms outstretched. As soon as she was close enough, he snagged her coat and hauled her out of the water, dragging her onto the dock beside him. A second later, Soldier was there too, his cold nose nudging her cheek.

"Jesus, she's gonna freeze," Van said. "Come on, boy." He leaped to his feet and picked her up, holding her tight against his chest. He hurried through the grass to his truck parked haphazardly in the parking lot. He set her on the passenger seat, then he ran around the truck and ripped

— Serena —

open the door. Soldier jumped in and Van followed, slamming the truck into gear, the tires kicking up dirt and gravel as he backed up and turned toward the road. Serena's teeth chattered and her entire body shook as waves of exhaustion rolled over her. The heat in Van's truck wasn't enough to combat the cold seeping into her bones and taking over her body. He parked in his driveway, ripped open the passenger door, and hauled her out, holding her tight against his body. She buried her face against his chest, grateful for his warmth.

Van sprinted up the stairs and inside, pausing long enough to let Soldier in and to kick the door closed behind him.

"What the hell were you thinking? Walking on the dock in this weather. Jesus, Serena, you're lucky I saw you walking down the road, or you'd be dead. You scared the shit out of me." He set her on the floor in front of the fire and kneeled beside her. "We have to get you warm, okay?"

Serena nodded, unable to speak, her throat raw and frozen, her jaw aching thanks to her chattering teeth.

"Yeah, well, you might not be so cool with it when I take off your clothes. I gotta get you out of your wet clothes. Are we still good?"

"D-do it, d-d-d-dammit," she stuttered.

Van stripped off her clothes—jacket, sweater, boots, and jeans—leaving her in her bra and panties. He grabbed a faded quilt from the back of the couch and wrapped it around her. He stood up long enough to take off his jacket and kick off his shoes, then he threw another log on the fire and sat down beside Serena, his arm around her.

She rested her head on his shoulder and looked up at him. "Th-th-thank you," she said. A chill raced through her, the shivering intensifying.

"Thank me when you warm up. You're still trembling, and your skin is ice cold." He glanced around the room and pushed himself to his feet with an angry huff. "I'll be right back."

He disappeared up the stairs. Serena could hear drawers opening and closing and Van muttering curses. Soldier crept closer to her until his head rested against her leg. He stared up at her with his big brown eyes and whined.

Serena rested her hand on Soldier's head. "G-good b-b-boy." If it weren't for him, she'd be dead. She squeezed her eyes closed. She couldn't think about that right now.

The stairs creaked as Van came back down. He dropped another blanket, a sweatshirt, and two huge towels on the floor beside her. He'd changed into a pair of gray sweats and a plain black t-shirt, wool socks on his feet. He sat down behind her, took hold of her hips and pulled her between his legs, her back against his chest. He picked up a towel and dried her hair as best he could, then he helped her put on a heavy University of Montana sweatshirt.

"Come here, boy," he ordered, snapping his fingers until Soldier wearily pushed himself to his feet and trudged closer to his master. Van used the second towel to dry off the dog, then he ordered him to lie down before he pulled another blanket over Serena's legs and wrapped his arms around her waist.

Serena dragged in a deep breath. It hurt. Soldier nudged her hand with his nose, so she adjusted the blanket to cover him.

Van chuckled. "I'm sure he appreciates that."

— *Serena* —

"He saved my life," she rasped. She tried to clear her throat, but it hurt too much. "He can have anything he wants."

"Yes, he can," Van agreed.

Serena turned on her side and laid her cheek on Van's chest. She closed her eyes and relaxed, safe in Van's arms. His grip on her never loosened; he kept her tucked tight against his chest, his hands splayed across her back.

Chapter Eight

Van

Van dragged in a deep breath and squeezed his eyes closed. He held Serena close, rubbing circles on her back, holding her tight. He refused to think about what had happened. He'd come too close to losing her.

"Van?" she murmured.

"You shouldn't talk. You need to rest."

She shook her head. "What did you mean?"

"What?"

"You said I scared you. Why?"

Van tucked her wet hair behind her ear and kissed her temple. "I thought I lost you. The thought of losing you when I just found you—it terrified me." He pressed another kiss to her temple, his lips lingering. "I promised to protect you no matter what and instead, I almost lost you because of a damn storm—"

"It was stupid to go out on the dock," Serena interrupted. "I wasn't thinking. I'm so sorry."

"All that matters is you're all right," Van insisted. He took hold of her chin and tipped her head back, forcing her to look at him. "Don't scare me again." He brushed a kiss across her lips.

Serena stared up at him, her cerulean blue eyes staring right into the depths of his soul. He swallowed back the fear struggling to take him over, to devour him.

"Van? What's wrong?"

He shook his head. There weren't enough words to tell her what she'd done to him in the short time they'd known each other.

"I-I don't know," he mumbled.

Serena sat up and turned to look at him. "Do you know why I was out there, walking in the storm?" She inched closer to him. "I was out there thinking about you. About you and me." She grabbed his hands, holding them tight between hers.

"You and me, huh?"

"I don't know what to do, Van. I like you. I enjoy spending time with you. Our friendship makes me happy, happier than I've been in a long time. But I'm scared, too. Scared to let myself feel anything for anybody. I've been hurt, shit, more than hurt, I've been destroyed, terrorized, ripped to shreds." Tears glistened in her eyes. "I think you could help put me back together again."

Van closed his eyes and exhaled. "God, Serena, it's like you can read my mind. I've been feeling things for you I haven't felt since my wife died."

"Why didn't you tell me?"

"God knows I wanted to. So many things held me back. Guilt. Fear. Doubt. I wasn't sure you wanted me. But after I kissed you and you asked me to stay—" He shook his

— *Van* —

head and laughed. "You don't know how hard it was to walk away last night."

Serena surged forward and flung her arms around his neck, her mouth on his, the kiss desperate and needy.

Van returned the kiss, his fingers digging into her hips as he dragged her into his lap. "I want to make you whole again," he growled. "Let me make you whole again, baby."

"Yes." She nodded. "Jesus, yes. Please."

He kissed her lips, her cheek, moving down her jaw and her neck to her shoulder, her skin still ice cold. He hooked a finger in the sweatshirt's collar, pulling it aside and sucking gently where her neck and shoulder met. Serena's eyes closed, her head fell back, and her body relaxed under his touch.

Van slid his hands up her bare thighs, under the edge of the sweatshirt, pushing it up and off. Serena shivered. He ran his hands up and down her arms as he continued kissing her.

"Are you still cold?" he asked.

"Yes." She sighed. "Sorry."

"Stop apologizing, sweetheart," Van scolded. "You fell in freezing cold water less than an hour ago. It's going to take some time to warm up."

Serena grabbed the front of his t-shirt and pulled him down on the floor on top of her. "You could warm me up." She tipped her chin and pursed her lips, nodding at him, an invitation.

Jesus, she was going to kill him. She laid beneath him, her damp hair fanned out around her, a smirk on her face, and complete trust in her eyes. Van kissed her, exploring her mouth with his tongue, his fingers skimming over her bare skin, memorizing her perfect body. Goosebumps rose on her skin everywhere he touched, everywhere he kissed, her body trembling under his hands.

Her fingers tangled in his hair, urging him back to her lips. She moaned into his mouth, the sound shooting straight to his cock. He let out an answering groan, his entire body on fire with need for this woman. His lips roamed over her body—her breasts, her stomach, her hips. He kissed a trail up her legs, stopping to knead, lick, and suck her inner thighs. Serena's hips thrust forward, chasing his mouth, but he wasn't ready yet; he wanted to take his time with her, savor her.

Van took her hands, holding them at her sides as he worked his way up her almost naked body—kissing her stomach, licking the soft mounds of her breasts, his tongue dancing over the lace covering her nipples. He nipped the sensitive skin of her neck before catching her lips in his, pushing his tongue into her mouth to kiss her again.

"Van," she gasped when he pulled away. She trembled, her fingers digging into his hips, her breath tearing in and out of her throat. Her eyes were dark with lust, her lips swollen from his kisses.

He couldn't get enough of her; it might never be enough. He reached behind her to unhook her bra, sliding it down her arms, his lips trailing after it. He tossed it aside and took her breast in his mouth, suckling it.

"God, you're so beautiful," Van growled. "I want you so bad, sweetheart."

Serena nodded and tugged his hair, pulling him to her mouth, kissing him. "Yes, Van," she moaned. "God, yes."

Van scrambled to his feet and yanked off his clothes, then he dropped to his knees and pulled Serena's lacy black panties down her legs, his lips once again on her stomach.

— *Van* —

He settled himself over her, his head between her legs. He had to taste her.

"Van, what are you doing?"

"I want you, sweetheart. I want to taste every inch of you."

Serena gasped and squeezed her eyes closed, her head shaking from side to side. "I-I don't know. I've never—"

Her mouth snapped shut with an audible click when Van flattened his tongue and slowly ran it along her silken folds. He groaned as her taste flooded his mouth. Something snapped inside of him, his control slipping. He dove in, burying his tongue and two fingers in her pussy, desperate for more, desperate to give her as much pleasure as he could. He lost himself in her, lost himself in the sounds she made, the gasps and moans, the way her body moved, her hips rising to meet his mouth, her hands clenched in the blankets beneath her. Her chest rose and fell, her breathing ragged until she screamed her pleasure as she came in his mouth and on his fingers.

Van held her, lapping at her soaking wet pussy, his finger brushing her swollen clit until she collapsed in a boneless, out of breath mess. He kissed her stomach, sloppy, wet kisses that made her giggle as he moved back up her body and buried his face against the side of her neck.

"Shit," he muttered. "I don't have any condoms."

"I'm on the pill," Serena replied. "I trust you."

"Are you sure?" he whispered, his lips brushing against her ear.

"I need you, Van. Make love to me. Please."

Van didn't hesitate. He pulled her legs around his waist and slid into her, almost coming from the feel of her warm heat surrounding him. He clenched his jaw, groaning as she writhed beneath him. His cock ached with the need to fuck her senseless. He closed his eyes, his hips flexing, moving carefully, afraid of hurting her, afraid he wouldn't be able to control himself.

Fingers tangled in his hair and soft lips moved over his neck. "Don't stop." Serena sighed. "I want this. I want *you*."

That was all he needed. His restraint, his self-control, vanished at those words. He slammed into her, burying himself deep, her hips rising to meet his. Tangled together, bodies moving, hips thrusting, lips crashing together, breath mingling, indistinct murmurs of praise and reassurance coming from them. She dragged her nails down his back, marking him as another orgasm consumed her, her body thrashing with pleasure. Her name rumbled from his chest as he came, her walls clenching around him, milking his cock dry.

They collapsed together in front of the fire, wrapped around each other, exchanging kisses. Van brushed her hair away from her face, reveling in her beauty. He couldn't stop kissing her; she was too good to be true. He was afraid to move, afraid this would end up being some beautiful dream he would wake up from and she would be gone.

"Is this real?" Serena whispered, echoing his thoughts.

"It is." Van chuckled. "Doesn't feel like it, though, does it?"

A tear slid down Serena's cheek. He brushed it away with his thumb. "What is it?"

She shrugged. "It's nothing. I'm...I'm happy, I guess. For the first time in forever, I'm not afraid."

Van kissed her, hugging her close. "As long as you're with me, you don't have to be afraid. I promised to protect you, and I meant it."

— *Van* —

Serena nodded. She rested her hand on his cheek and smiled. "Thank you, Van. For everything." She snuggled close to him, her head resting on his chest.

Van covered Serena with the quilt, brushed the hair from her forehead, and grabbed his phone from the table. Soldier opened one eye, huffed, and rolled to his back, bumping into Serena. She didn't move.

He took his phone and went up the stairs, ducking into his bedroom and pushing the door closed behind himself. He hit the button to call Lincoln, put the phone to his ear, and waited.

"Loser!" Lincoln greeted him. "What's up?"

"Hey, asshole." Van chuckled. "I need a favor. I need you to investigate someone for me. I don't have much information though."

"Hold on." Van could hear shuffling and grunting, Lincoln muttered something, and someone responded. "Alright, go ahead."

"His name is Trace. I don't have a last name."

"How the hell am I supposed to find some guy without a last name?" Lincoln grumbled.

"He lived with Serena. Find him through her."

"What's going on? Who is this guy?"

"It's her ex and the reason she's in Montana. He was abusive. I think it goes deeper than that. I want to know how deep. So, find any guy named Trace connected to Serena Chasey. They lived in California when they started dating."

"Is that all you know?" Lincoln asked.

"It is. I know it's not a lot to go on, but I want as much info as you can get me. Especially a current location, any restraining orders, reciprocity with Montana, anything you can find out." Van scrubbed a hand over his face. Always start with information: the more you knew about the enemy, the better equipped you were to handle him when confronted.

"Is Serena okay? Are you?"

"We're both fine. I'll be even better once you get me what I need. I can't protect her if I don't know what I'm going up against."

"Should I be worried?" his best friend asked.

"Not yet. I'm trying to be cautious."

"Does this mean what I think it means?"

Van laughed. "It might. You know I don't kiss and tell."

Lincoln let out a loud whoop. "You told me everything I need to know. Thank God. I knew there was something about her I liked. She is a gift, dude, and you better treat her like one. I like her. A lot."

"Yeah, so do I. And for some crazy reason, she likes me. Get back to me as soon as you can. I gotta go." Van disconnected the call before Lincoln could ask him any more questions. He wanted to get back downstairs to Serena.

She was still under the covers, the top of her head visible, Soldier curled up beside her. Van stepped into the kitchen and started a pot of coffee, then he poured some food into Soldier's bowl. The dog's head popped up at the sound, and he slowly padded into the kitchen, stopping to stretch beside his master.

Van crouched beside him and smoothed his fur, checking him over for any injuries. He'd been so concerned with Serena he'd forgotten Soldier had dived

— *Van* —

into the ice-cold water, too. The dog seemed none the worse for wear.

"You're a good boy, buddy," Van praised. "Good job today."

Soldier licked Van's cheek and yipped quietly as if he agreed. Van scratched behind his ears one more time before rising to his feet and gesturing for Soldier to eat.

"Do I smell coffee?" Serena mumbled from the floor.

Van crossed the room in two long strides, dropping to the floor beside her and gathering her in his arms. He caught her lips in his and kissed her, her arms coming up around his neck as he crushed her to his chest.

"Hi," she murmured when he released her.

"Hi." He grinned. "You hungry?"

"Starving." She extricated herself from his grip and grabbed the sweatshirt from the floor, tugging it on.

Van helped her to her feet, the sweatshirt falling almost to her knees. He pulled her back into his arms and kissed her again.

"I could get used to this." Serena sighed.

"So could I," he agreed. "Come on. I've got some coffee cake in the fridge. Let's get some food in you."

Serena nodded, her hand in his as he led her to the kitchen. He could definitely get used to this.

Chapter Nine

Serena

Dating Van was easy, simple. Pure. He cared about her, that much she knew, but he didn't burden her with the knowledge. Trace had used his love for her—if you could call it love—like a weapon, wielding it like a sword, holding it over her like an executioner preparing to remove her head from her body.

Is it possible to fall in love with someone in less than week? Because she thought she might be falling in love with Van. She thought falling in love again would frighten her; fear kept her from ever going down that road again. For Serena, love was abuse, love was terrifying, love was pain.

Van was the opposite of all the bad she'd known. He demanded nothing of her and gave her everything in return. She was happier than she ever thought possible. She felt free, content, *alive*.

"Earth to Serena," Van whispered, squeezing the hand he held in his. "You okay over there, sweetheart?"

"Yeah, sorry." She laughed. "Lost in thought." She turned to face him, tucking her foot under her leg. "Did I tell you thank you for this? Going to this faculty thing with me, I mean."

Van kissed the back of her hand. "You can thank me later." He chuckled.

Serena laughed and nodded. God, he made her feel good. "Oh, I will, trust me."

The "faculty thing" was a faculty party at Charles Ross's house. Every year, Charlie had an enormous dinner party for everyone who worked at the university. He claimed it was the one time of year he could get all the staff together under one roof. Ross wouldn't take no for an answer: everybody came, no excuses. He promised Serena if she showed up for this one party, he wouldn't bother her again for another year.

When she'd told Van about it, he'd offered to go with her. She hadn't even had to ask. She'd thrown her arms around him and kissed him, which had led to a satisfying round of sex up against the wall in his living room. That had been his first thank you. The other would come later tonight after they got home.

Van followed Serena's directions, coming to a stop in front of a huge three-story house on the edge of the lake. He whistled as he put the truck in gear and peered through the windshield at the brightly lit home.

"This is impressive," he said.

"Wow," Serena breathed. "I'm under-dressed for a place like this."

"You look gorgeous," Van told her. He gave her hand a tug, urging her closer. She slid across the seat, into his arms. He kissed her, his hand sliding up her leg, under her skirt.

Serena slapped his hand and nipped at his lower lip. "Later," she laughed.

Van groaned, pushed open the truck door, and helped Serena out. He wrapped his arm around her waist and led her to the front door. He tugged at the collar of his shirt, grimacing. Serena pushed his hand away and straightened his collar.

"You look great."

"I hate dress shirts. And jackets," he grumbled. "You're lucky I like you."

"More than lucky." Serena smiled, pressing a kiss to the corner of his mouth. "Blessed."

The door opened and Charlie ushered them inside. Serena introduced him to Van, then they followed him through the foyer and down the hall to the back of the house. The living room opened to a patio and a vast yard sloping downhill and right up to the edge of the lake. Strings of lights hung from the trees, portable heaters sat every ten feet, and fall foliage decorated the twenty-five tables at the edge of the patio.

Charlie showed them where the bar was, then he excused himself to greet more guests. A substantial crowd had gathered; some of them Serena knew, most of them she didn't. Even though Lakeside College was considered a small university, it had a large staff.

Serena greeted those she knew as they moved through the crowd, her hand in Van's. She stopped to hug Marcia and ask how retired life was treating her, she nodded hello to the town sheriff, Donna Willis, whom she'd met on a couple of occasions, and she waved at Professor Campbell and his best friend, Jacob, a young professor who would start at the university second semester.

They stopped at the bar where Serena got a glass of wine and Van got a beer, then they found an empty table and took a seat. Van slung his arm over the back of her chair, his fingers brushing her shoulder. Something so simple shouldn't have made her heart pound and heat rise in her cheeks. Knowing Van did it out of genuine affection rather than possessiveness presented a scenario she wasn't accustomed to.

Serena leaned into him and kissed the corner of his mouth, a smile dancing across her lips.

"What was that for?"

"For being you." She shrugged. "And for being so great. You make it easy."

"What do I make easy?" His arm slid off the back of the chair and circled her waist, his breath blew warm against her ear.

She almost told him how he made it easy to love him, but she bit her tongue and held back. Not now. Not yet.

"Everything," she said instead. "You make everything easy."

Serena had a great time. She'd worried they wouldn't have fun, that Van wouldn't, but those fears were laid to rest early in the evening. Van was quick to make friends; she was a bit surprised, considering how grumpy he'd seemed when they first met, but he was jovial and easygoing. He chatted with her colleagues like they were old friends, accepted invites to go fishing or off-roading. He even agreed to look at Charlie's ailing boat.

Food, drink, and dancing consumed the evening. Van twirled her around the dance floor and hummed quietly in her ear, his arms tight around her, holding her close as they danced to her favorite songs. She pinched herself several times to make sure she wasn't dreaming.

They were one of the last to leave, the party winding down after midnight. They chatted with another couple in the driveway for a few minutes, entertaining the notion of a couple's night out before saying their goodbyes and climbing into the truck. Van turned on the heat and pulled her against his side as they drove home. Serena rested her head on his shoulder, her hand on his leg, her face aching from smiling all night.

Van parked in his driveway, helped her from the truck, and led her across the street. She handed him the key to the condo and let him unlock her door. He paused outside the door.

"Aren't you coming in?" she asked.

"Was waiting for you to ask, sweetheart." He smirked, stepping across the threshold and pushing the door closed behind him.

Serena tossed her jacket over the chair and kicked off her boots. She sank onto the couch with a sigh, rested her head against the back, and closed her eyes.

Van sat down beside her, put his finger under her chin, tilted her head back, and kissed her, his tongue dancing across her lips until she opened her mouth, a breathy moan escaping her.

"I've been wanting to kiss you all night."

"I can't believe you waited so long," Serena mumbled.

"It took a lot of restraint." He chuckled. "I like your work friends."

"They liked you. A lot." She sat up, took his face in her hands, and kissed him, nipping at his lower lip. "Let's go in the bedroom."

Van laughed, gathered her in his arms, and carried her down the hall to the bedroom. She'd left the light on the bedside table burning—she always left a light on—so Van carried her inside and sat on the edge of the bed with her still in his arms. He held Serena tight as he stretched out across the bed, her head on his arm, his hand on her waist, his fingers under the edge of her sweater, cold against her skin.

Serena tucked herself against Van's side, her arm around his waist. He tangled his fingers in her hair, cupped her head in his hand, tugging her even closer. He took her leg and pulled it up over his, his leg between hers, his thigh grazing her center, his chest pressed to hers, his hand on her hip holding her in place. His kisses were soft, gentle, almost timid.

"You know I'm not breakable, right?" She giggled.

Van laughed, a breathy laugh that caused heat to pool in the pit of her stomach. "Oh, I know. But I want to take my time, sweetheart. Take you apart piece by piece."

Serena squeezed her eyes closed and groaned. Van slipped his hand under her sweater, his calloused fingers scratching at her skin as he stroked her waist. This time the kiss was deep, needy, scorching. He cupped her breast, circling her nipple with his finger, bringing it to a hard peak.

She gasped and arched into his hand. Van was always gentle, treating her with reverence and care, making her feel so special and so wanted even a simple touch pushed her to the edge.

"Is this okay?" he whispered against her mouth, his breath mingling with hers, his finger repeatedly brushing over the hard pebble of her nipple.

"God, yes," Serena moaned.

He rolled her to her back, settling himself between her legs, his mouth and hands touching and caressing her all over. Van's hips rocked into hers, the hard line of his erection pressing into her aching core. Serena squirmed beneath him, desperate for more. She slipped her hand between them and rubbed him through the thick fabric of his jeans. He groaned into her mouth, his tongue vibrating against hers, sending tingles of pleasure shooting through her.

"Mm, Jesus, Serena," he murmured. He pulled her sweater off, his lips moving down her neck and across her chest. "I want to feel your skin against mine, beautiful."

He slipped off her bra, lifting her effortlessly to toss it aside before he mouthed her tight, hard nipple, his tongue dancing and flitting over her breasts. She held the back of his head as his hot, wet mouth closed over her breast, making her heady with desire.

Serena twisted her fingers in the back of his shirt and tugged, wanting the same thing he wanted, skin on skin.

Van sat up between her legs, pulled off his shirt and unbuttoned his jeans before returning to his position between her legs. His bare chest pressed against hers, his hips flexing into hers, the button from his jeans scratching her bare stomach. Serena ran her hands up and down his back and sides, examining every inch of his bare skin. She rained kisses across his chest, her tongue flicking out to lick at the hollow of his throat, kissing every freckle, mark, and mole gracing his neck and torso. Her fingers danced over his back, sliding into the belt loops on his jeans so she could pull him into her.

The sound of their desire fused into one sound—a gasp and a moan, the shuffling of clothes being removed, skin sliding against skin—whispers of things to come. Every touch filled with want and need, every kiss a promise, every sound a symphony of lust.

Serena's body screamed for attention, for Van. She took him in her hand, stroking him, her hand sliding along his shaft, her thumb drifting over the head of his cock.

Van moved to her side, his hand drifting up her thighs, pushing her legs open, his fingers slipping into her folds, caressing her, his lips at her throat, suckling. He slid one finger inside her, taking his time, exploring her carefully. He cupped her, his palm resting on her clit, massaging it with the heel of his hand, until she was bucking and writhing, begging him to let her come. He pressed his mouth to her ear, words of praise and encouragement filling Serena's head as she orgasmed under his expert touch, arching so far off the bed the only thing touching it were her feet and head, her hands clutching desperately at his arm.

Serena fell back to the bed, wrung out, her breath tearing in and out of her throat, her skin hot and flushed. Van's hand stayed between her legs, his lips sliding down her cheek to her mouth, sucking her tongue into his mouth, moaning deep in the back of his throat, his cock hard against her hip.

She pushed him to his back and took his head in her hands, deepening the kiss. Van held his cock in his hand as she lowered herself onto him, his hips tilting up as she rocked back and forth until he was fully seated.

"Fuck, Serena. I need you to move, sweetheart," Van groaned. His hands were tight on her hips, his calloused fingertips biting into her skin as he held her, tugging her forward, urging her to move.

She leaned over him, her hands on either side of his head, her knees digging into the bed beside his hips. She moved, pushing herself down onto him, then sliding up his cock, holding the tip inside of her.

"Oh shit, that's what I want," Van growled, his head thrown back, droplets of sweat beaded on his forehead. His hips snapped up to meet hers, his thrusts hard and deep, the two of them moving faster and faster, racing toward their inevitable finish. Van thrust up one last time, his entire body tense, his cock throbbing as he came.

His fingers caressed her clit and then she joined him, her entire body alight with pleasure as she came, head thrown back, eyes closed, Van's name a curse on her lips.

Van pulled her down onto his chest and brushed her hair away from her face before placing a gentle kiss to her forehead. He pulled the blankets over her, wrapped his arms around her and held her close, his chin resting on the top of her head, his breathing steady and even as he drifted off to sleep.

Chapter Ten

Van

She kissed him on the corner, damn the paparazzi, before she laughed and skipped up the street, smiling back at him and waving over her shoulder. He couldn't help but smile, her enthusiasm contagious as always. He shouted after her to wait, but she ducked into the coffee shop, her laughter floating back to him, sweet and vibrant over the sound of the busy New York streets.

Van sighed. What was the point of a bodyguard if she wouldn't let him protect her?

The first scream he heard wasn't hers, but it had him shoving the street vendor who'd stopped him out of the way and darting through the crowd, knocking aside the shocked bystanders. He reached her just as Trace dropped the match, the gas igniting with a giant whoosh that knocked the air out of him and sent him stumbling backward. He threw himself at her, the fingers of his left hand twisting in her blouse, the flames dancing up his arm—

"Serena!" he screamed.

"Van." A hand settled on his arm, cooling the heat flickering below his elbow. "Van. Look at me." Dark blue eyes locked on his, her chest pressed against his, her weight comforting, familiar. She exhaled, her breath warm against his skin.

His gaze held hers, and his hands settled on her waist. He inhaled, her scent filling his head, clearing the phantom stench of burning flesh. He cupped the back of her head, caught her lips in his, and kissed her breathless.

"Hey, you okay?" she asked when he released her. "You scared me."

"Sorry." He sighed, tucking her hair behind her ear. "Bad dream."

"Do you want to talk about it?"

"Not really," he said. "I've never been much of one to talk about personal stuff. Except with my shrink and the last time I saw him was about six or seven months ago."

"You can talk to me, Van. I *want* you to talk to me. If this is going to work—"

"We need to talk," he finished. "I know." Van sat up, leaned against the headboard, and pulled Serena between his legs, her back against his chest. He took her hands, his fingers intertwined with hers, resting on her stomach. He kissed her neck.

"Can I tell you something? Something that might freak you out?"

"Go ahead," Serena said. She squeezed his hands a little too tight.

"After Adelaide died, I was destroyed. Devastated. I came to Montana to hide, to leave the world behind, hoping it would forget about me and leave me to die,

— *Van* —

alone and miserable. Linc wouldn't let that happen. He kept bugging me, coming out here, refusing to leave me alone. He wouldn't give up on me."

"Thank God for Lincoln," she commented.

Van chuckled. "Then he had the audacity to bring a beautiful, enticing, mysterious woman to dinner at my place. And I fell for her. And I keep falling for her more and more every day. I've fallen so hard it's kind of scary how strong my feelings have become in such a short time. Scary and crazy."

Serena shook her head, a shaky breath leaving her. "If you're crazy, so am I." She tipped her head back to look at him. "It is scary, isn't it? I want to let myself go, let myself fall in love with you, Van, but I'm scared." A tear trickled down her cheek. "The last time I loved someone, I got hurt."

Van cupped her cheek and brushed away the tear with his thumb. "I will never hurt you. I promise." His lips drifted over hers. "And I won't let anyone hurt you, either. I love you, sweetheart."

"I love you, too," she whispered.

Van pulled her into his lap, their lips smashing together, tongues tangling. They broke apart, gasping for air. Serena pushed the blankets off him, her lips back on his, her hands all over him, running down his back, over his stomach and between his legs, taking his cock in her hands, her thumb smearing the pre-cum across the tip and down the length, stroking him roughly. She grabbed his hand and pulled it between her legs.

"Touch me," she moaned. "I need you to touch me, Van."

He did as she asked, his fingers grazing the lips of her pussy, seeking and finding her clit, circling it, smirking when her hips jerked under his touch, and she groaned into his mouth. The sound made his dick rock hard, achingly hard.

His need for her was off the charts, insane, scary, *crazy*. This woman woke something deep within him that had been lying dormant since Adelaide's death. He wanted her, needed her, ached for her. He had to have her. All of her, forever.

Serena broke off the kiss and slid down his body, kissed her way until she was nestled between his legs, his cock in her hand, her lips brushing it, her breath blowing over him. Van groaned and his fingers twisted in her hair as she slid him into her mouth, taking him until his cock hit the back of her throat. It constricted around him, and he nearly lost it.

"Fuck, sweetheart," he gasped, his hips rising to push himself deeper into her mouth, her hands splayed over his thighs, squeezing and releasing, her head bobbing as she worked him over, sucking and licking. He was close, so fucking close. His breath tore out of his throat, and his heart pounded in his chest, his balls drawn up tight, his stomach jumping in anticipation.

She released him before he came, moving to straddle him again, lowering herself onto his cock, rocking forward, leaning over to catch his lips in hers, kissing him. Van planted his feet on the bed, his hands on her waist, holding her in place as he thrust deep inside her. She moaned, the sound unbelievably sexy, unbelievably perfect. He wanted to be the only one to pull those sounds from her, the only one to make her moan, to make her cry out his name. He wanted to be hers forever.

He pulled Serena down on his chest, rolled her to her back, his cock still inside of her, his hips flexing, her legs

— Van —

wrapped around his waist as he pounded into her. She clawed at his back, her voice rising in a crescendo of yeses as he pushed her closer and closer to orgasm until she called his name as she came, her perfect skin flushed, sweat on her brow, her body convulsing around him.

He let out a long, stuttering groan as her walls tightened around his cock and her nails dug into his shoulders, his own orgasm pushing every thought, every doubt out of his mind, the only thing was Serena, her body, her scent, her taste on his tongue, those glorious sounds echoing in his ears. He collapsed on top of her, his lips on hers, consumed with her. She was his everything.

He never thought he could love again, but Serena changed all that. Serena healed him.

Van tossed the file and photos on the table and pushed a hand through his hair. Lincoln had sent the file as soon as he could, everything he could find on Trace Alvers. Thirty, well-educated, came from a privileged background. Serena had a standing restraining order against him, issued in California, but one that would likely hold up in a Montana court if needed. He had three separate assault charges—two while in college, ex-girlfriends, and one pending in Arizona—along with several DUIs. Lincoln got his juvenile records unsealed, and they discovered he'd put a girl in the hospital after she'd broken up with him. His parents had buried it, and Trace had gotten nothing more than community service.

The man had a history, one Van didn't like. It made him sick to his stomach to read about all the people—all the women—Trace had hurt. There was no telling what lengths he would go to in order to get Serena back.

His phone chirped, a text from his shrink, reminding him of his appointment on Wednesday, an appointment he no longer wanted to keep. The last thing he wanted to do was go out of town and leave Serena alone.

Van hadn't seen his therapist in six months, ever since he'd packed up his practice and moved to Missoula. Dr. Sadler had been calling and emailing for two solid months, reminding Van he needed to pay him a visit. He'd agreed to drive down and meet with him, if only to get Sadler off his back.

He regretted it now, especially after reading Trace's file. An uneasy feeling had settled over him the last few days; something wasn't right. He couldn't put his finger on it, but his hunches were rarely wrong. He was unsettled. If he'd paid attention to this same feeling before Adelaide's death, he wouldn't have lost her.

He tried to cancel a few days ago, but Sadler refused to hear of it.

"Get your ass down here, Van. We can talk about why you don't want to come when you're here."

Van reluctantly agreed and promised he'd see Sadler on Wednesday. He figured he'd drive to Missoula, visit Sadler, grab lunch, take care of some business needs for Lincoln, visit Soldier's vet, and head back home. Hopefully, he'd be gone no more than eight or nine hours.

At least Serena would be at work all day, safe at the university. It wouldn't stop him from worrying about her.

Van showed up at her door bright and early Wednesday morning, carrying two coffees in metal tumblers along with a box of donuts. Serena had playfully pouted when

— *Van* —

he'd told her about his brief trip, teasing that she couldn't last one day without him. He'd promised to bring her breakfast and kiss her goodbye before he left.

Hands full, he tapped on the door with his foot. When she didn't answer right away, he looked at Soldier.

"Soldier, *een rede houden*."

Soldier barked twice and scratched at the door. After a few seconds, Serena yanked the door open, still in her pajamas, her hair in a ponytail on top of her head. She gestured for them to come in, a huge grin spreading across her face when Van put the tumbler of coffee in her hand.

"You are a life saver, babe," she sighed.

Soldier leaned against her legs and stared up at her. Van thought the dog might love her more than his owner. She rubbed his head, scratching behind his ears. Soldier's tongue lolled out the side of his mouth, and if he could have purred like a cat, Van was sure he would have.

"You should leave him here with me."

Van shook his head. "I'm sure he'd love to stay here, but I don't know how Charlie would feel about you taking a dog to work."

"Charlie wouldn't care." Serena shrugged. "Come on. Please?"

It wasn't a bad idea. Leaving Soldier with Serena for the day would certainly help with his anxiety. Soldier would protect her with his life.

"Okay." He narrowed his eyes. "Promise you'll take care of him?"

"Of course, I will." She grinned. "Soldier, *ga liggen*." The dog padded to the corner where Serena had put a blanket for him and laid down.

"You're getting better at Dutch," Van said.

"Lots of practice." She stepped close to Van and looked up at him. "Are you sure you'll be back tonight? I heard there was a storm moving in. It might make driving back difficult."

He kissed the tip of her nose. "I'll be fine." He wrapped his arm around her and pulled her flush against him. "I'll come over when I get home."

"You better. I'll be waiting. Don't leave me hanging." She brushed her fingers through his hair and pulled him down to kiss her. "Promise me you'll be careful."

"I wish you could come with me."

"God, I'm tempted. But Charlie has a meeting with the board of regents on Friday, and we have a lot of work to do before then. I can't go."

Van rested his forehead against hers and closed his eyes. "I know." He sighed.

"What's wrong?" she asked.

"I don't know." He shrugged. "I have a bad feeling I can't shake. It's eating at me. Just...promise me you'll be careful, okay?"

Serena nodded. "I will. Besides, I have Soldier. He'll take care of me." She pushed up on her toes, her lips on his. "Do you think you'll be back in time for dinner?"

"I'll try."

Her blue eyes sparkled, and she smirked. "Try really hard. I can guarantee you'll love what's for dessert."

Van growled low in the back of his throat, crushed her to his chest, and rained kisses over her face and throat. "Fuck, sweetheart, I think I'll have to do more than try." His pulse raced and his head spun. This woman drove him crazy and he loved it.

— *Van* —

    Serena walked him, to his truck, kissed him goodbye, and made him promise to text her when he got to Missoula and again when he left. He rolled the window down and waved as he pulled away, watching her in the rearview mirror until she went inside.

Chapter Eleven

Serena

Serena took her time getting ready. Thanks to Van, she was up early, far earlier than normal. She didn't mind; she would have been upset with him if he hadn't stopped to tell her goodbye before he left.

She couldn't wipe the smile from her face. She was in love, and she wanted to shout it from the top of the Mission Mountains. Her life was on the right track after years of derailment. It was time to leave Trace in her past where he belonged and embrace her future with Van.

She showed up early for work, Soldier in tow, made coffee, and got the office ready for the day, singing under her breath as she worked.

Her good mood and cheesy, lovestruck grin did not go unnoticed. Charlie mentioned it when he came in, Professor Campbell mentioned it when he stopped by, even a couple of students teased her during lunch in the student union. She laughed and brushed them off, joking with them for a few minutes before she sat in the corner with her food and a book she'd grabbed from the library. Soldier laid on the floor at her feet, gazing up at her.

Halfway through her lunch, an uneasy feeling came over her. Serena couldn't put her finger on it, couldn't figure out what bothered her; she felt *wrong*. She laid her book on the table and looked around the room.

A couple sat a few tables away from her, completely engrossed with each other. On the other side of the room, a young man was studying at a table by the wall. There were several students in line for food and several professors. Nothing seemed out of the ordinary, but something was off. Serena tucked her book under her arm, ordered Soldier to follow her, and hurried from the student union. She couldn't shake the feeling someone was watching her. She picked up the pace until she and Soldier were sprinting across campus and into the office. At least Charlie wasn't there; she didn't have to explain her flushed cheeks and heavy breathing. It was ridiculous to even think someone might have been following her.

Serena dropped into her chair, her head in her hands. She was paranoid. Things were going well and that meant any minute, it could go bad. Over the last two years, any time her life seemed to get back on track—new job, new home, anything good—Trace had swooped in and yanked it out from under her. It made sense she worried it would happen again, especially since she'd found Van. The thought of having it torn away, having Van torn away, terrified her. It was her imagination and the fear she'd continually lived with for two years playing tricks with her head.

— *Serena* —

Her phone vibrated on the desk beside her, making her jump and squeal. Startled, Soldier growled quietly, his ears up. Serena snatched up her phone, frowning.

[Van: Hey, sweetheart. I might not make it back by dinner. Some stuff came up that put me behind. I'll text when I leave.]

She sighed and pushed a hand through her hair. His absence fueled her paranoia. She'd gotten too used to having Van around. She missed him, needed him.

"The woes of being in love," she muttered under her breath. She couldn't help but laugh at herself. Most days she felt like she was having an out of body experience; it didn't seem real, the way she felt about Van or the way her life had changed in a short time. Serena had come to Montana to start over, and it was exactly what she had done. She'd hit the reset button and got a second chance at love.

Being in love with Van was so different than what she'd had with Trace. Now that she knew what genuine love felt like, she wondered if she'd ever been in love with Trace or in love with the *idea* of being in love with Trace. He'd been her entire world because he'd forced her to make him her entire world.

Footsteps running down the hall outside the office drew her from her musings. Soldier jumped to his feet and faced the door, his hackles up, another low growl leaving him. Her back stiffened and a sense of dread washed over her. She stared at the door, expecting it to burst open and Trace to be standing on the other side.

After a few seconds, Soldier backed away from the door and came to sit beside Serena's chair. He put his paw on her leg and stared at her with his big brown eyes.

"Good boy, Soldier." She wrapped her arm around his neck and chastised herself; it was probably a student late for class. She had to shake this feeling of being watched before it drove her insane.

The door opened and Charlie marched in, barking orders as soon as he stepped into the room. She grabbed her notepad and started scribbling notes as she followed Charlie into his office, Soldier on her heels.

If Van were going to be later than expected, she might as well stay at work and get some stuff done. Fortunately, she had a lot to do. She still had the paper to type up and the power point presentation to put together before Friday. If she got it done now, she might not have to work late on Thursday.

It was after seven when Serena pulled through the security gate. Van's truck wasn't behind the condo or in his driveway, which meant he wasn't back from Missoula yet. He'd texted her over an hour ago and said he was on his way home, giving her enough time to leave work, run by the condo to drop off Soldier, go grab some groceries, and get back home. He promised to come over as soon as he got back, no matter how late it was. Thank God. She missed him.

She parked next to her condo, climbed out of the car, and got Soldier from Van's condo. Out of the corner of her eye she noticed the light in her kitchen shining through the glass in the door. She thought she'd turned it off when she left for work; then again, she could be mistaken. Her head had been in the clouds, her lips still burning from Van's goodbye kiss. It was possible she'd forgotten to turn it off.

"Soldier, *zitten*," she ordered while she dug through her purse for her keys.

She stuck her key in the door, but to her surprise, it wasn't locked. She'd been diligent about locking it ever since Van scolded her about it. Her head must have been so far in the clouds this morning she'd forgotten. She pushed it open and reached for the light.

A rough, calloused hand wrapped around her upper arm and yanked her backward, her purse and jacket falling to the floor. The door slammed closed, leaving the dog outside. He immediately started barking. A startled squeak escaped her before a huge, clammy hand covered her mouth. The odor of stale whiskey and a familiar, expensive cologne washed over her.

"Hey, darlin'," A deep voice growled in her ear. "I've been looking for you."

Her gorge rose and her entire body went cold, goosebumps breaking out all over her. Tears gathered at the corner of her eyes and fear constricted her heart like a vise.

Trace.

Panic set in; she struggled to get away, kicking her feet and flailing her arms. Her elbow connected with his sternum, and he released her with a loud grunt. She threw herself forward and fell to her knees, crawled across the floor, and pressed her back against the kitchen cabinet, eyes darting around, looking for a way to escape. Trace stalked across the room and crouched in front of her, his hand pressed to his chest, rubbing the spot she'd hit, his face unreadable. He reached for her, and she flinched, bracing herself for the blow she knew was coming.

But Trace didn't hit her. His touch was surprisingly gentle, his finger drifting down her cheekbone. "God, I missed you," he murmured. "You're looking good, babe."

"Wh-what are you doing here, Trace?" she stammered, recoiling from his touch. "How did you...how did you find me?"

"I told you. I've been looking for you. It wasn't easy either. If you hadn't gotten the job at the university, I never would have been able to track you down."

"What? How?"

"Social security numbers, baby." Trace chuckled. "I tracked you here using your social security number. I knew where you worked, but it took me about a week to figure out where you lived. Took even longer to get you alone." He leaned over her, his faces inches from hers. "I don't know who the hell that long-haired hippie you're fucking is, but it is over. You got your fun, but it's time you remembered who you belong to. You're coming home with me."

She wrenched away from him, scooting across the floor, trying to put some distance between her and Trace. He followed her, hovering over her, arms crossed, a scowl marring his features.

"No use running, baby. Get your ass off the floor and go pack. Don't make me tell you again."

Serena burst into tears, heaving sobs tearing through her body, doubling her over. She gnawed on her knuckle, trying to hold back the tears, but they wouldn't stop. It was like she was shedding her new life, her new love, shedding it as her tears hit the tile floor.

Trace leaned against the counter, watching her, disgust written all over his face. It wasn't until her sobs subsided that he spoke.

"Are you done?" he asked. "Fuck me. Get moving. We're leaving. I hate these damn small towns. I can feel the redneck creeping up on me as we speak."

"No." Serena grabbed the edge of the counter and pulled herself to her feet. There was no way in hell she was leaving with Trace. Not in a million years. She straightened her shoulders and stared up at him.

"I'm not going anywhere with you," she told him, praying her voice wouldn't betray her fear. "Get the hell out of my house."

The slap knocked her into the counter, her lower back connecting with the edge, sending a sharp pain up her spine. She gasped and gripped the handle of the stove so hard her knuckles turned white. Fresh tears spilled down her cheeks.

Trace sighed and shook his head. "I don't know who the fuck you think you're talking to, Serena, but you better get your goddamn head on straight." He stabbed a finger toward the door. "I am walking out the door in five minutes. You can go voluntarily, or I can carry you over my shoulder. Either way, I'm leaving, and you are, too."

"Trace, stop!" she cried, shaking her head. "You have to stop. I am not going anywhere with you. I don't love you. It's over, and it has been for a long time. Get out of my house. Now."

This time he backhanded her, her head whipping to the side, her lip splitting, the coppery taste of blood flooding her mouth. She stumbled, clinging to the counter, desperate to stay on her feet, desperate to show him he would not intimidate her. She could hear Soldier barking outside; she prayed someone would hear him and come check on her.

"You little bitch," he seethed. "Why do you make me do that? Why do you have to make me angry? If you would do as I told you, I wouldn't have to hit you." He advanced until he was toe to toe with her, towering over her, his fists clenched at his sides, his face bright red, the vein in the center of his forehead throbbing. "Go pack your shit. I am not telling you again."

Lights splashed across the window, drawing Trace's attention away from her. Serena darted to the side and around him, running for the door. She had the doorknob in her hand when Trace grabbed her hair and yanked her to the floor. She screamed, the sound echoing through the house.

Trace hauled her to her feet and pushed her toward the bedroom, muttering obscenities under his breath. She stumbled into the wall, freezing in place at the sound of a knock on the door.

"Serena! You okay, sweetheart?"

"Fuck," Trace mumbled under his breath. He scrubbed a hand over his shaved head, grabbed Serena by the back of the neck, took the paring knife from the dish rack, and led her to the door. He pressed his mouth against her ear, squeezing her neck until she groaned.

"Open it and get rid of him. Or I will." He wiggled the knife in front of her face. "Understood?"

Serena nodded, took a deep breath, and opened the door to talk to Van.

Chapter Twelve
Van

The drive back to Lakeside from Missoula was a bitch. The storm started as soon as he hit the road, a thick, driving snow blanketing the ground within minutes. His need to rush, to hurry home to Serena, quelled thanks to the weather.

His visit with Dr. Sadler had gone better than he expected. His progress thrilled the doctor, especially when he heard Van was seeing someone. He'd tried to contain his excitement but had failed. Miserably. They'd spent the hour talking about Serena and Van's feelings for her. When he left Sadler's office, he felt better than he had in months.

It was almost eight when he pulled through the gate. He swung wide to pull into the driveway but to his surprise, the truck lights illuminated Soldier standing in the road between his condo and Serena's. He slammed on the brakes, threw the truck in park, and shoved open the door.

Van heard the scream as soon as he opened the truck door. Soldier heard it too because he spun around and raced to Serena's door, barking and growling before turning to look at his owner and whining loudly. He snatched his gun from the center console, tucked it into his waistband, and jogged down the road, whistling for Soldier to heel.

Serena's car was parked in her driveway, and her kitchen light was on. He went to the side door and knocked, three sharp raps on the glass. He tried to see inside, but the blinds covering the window were closed.

"Serena! You okay, sweetheart?"

He seriously considered breaking down the door, but before he could, Serena flung it open. Her eyes were red, her hair mussed and out of place. It looked like she'd been crying. Something was wrong.

"Hey," she mumbled.

"Are you okay?" Van asked.

"Yeah, I'm fine." Serena's eyes darted to the left, so quick he almost missed it, then back to him.

He put his hand on the door and one foot over the threshold, but Serena didn't move. She clung to the doorknob with both hands, gripping it tight. Soldier let out a low growl, his hackles raised, his body pressed against Van's leg.

"I...I had a crappy day. Charlie was an asshole all day, his usual self. Can I get a raincheck on dinner?"

A chill raced down Van's spine. Charlie was never an asshole; Serena had told him more than once Charles Ross was the kindest, sweetest, best boss she had ever had. He took a step back and cleared his throat.

"Sure, sweetheart. Call me if you change your mind."

— Van —

Serena nodded and slammed the door without another word. Van took another step back, closed his eyes, and counted to ten. Then he opened his eyes and raised his foot, connecting with the door right beneath the knob next to the jamb. The door flew open and hit the wall.

Serena stood in the center of the kitchen, a tall, burly bald man behind her. Van recognized him from the photos Lincoln had sent him. Trace. As soon as the door hit the wall, he wrapped an arm around Serena's neck and dragged her back against his body, a small paring knife pressed to the underside of her chin.

Van's heart pounded, hard enough to hurt. If he weren't careful, he would lose Serena, like he'd lost Adelaide. He couldn't let that happen.

"Let her go," Van growled.

"Fuck you," Trace shot back. "She's mine. You had your fun with her, but now it's over. Tuck your dick back in your pants and haul ass back across the street. She's coming home with me."

Soldier growled at Van's feet; his fur stood on end and he crouched, ready to spring. Van held out his hand, silently ordering him to stay.

"I'm not fucking around, Trace. Let her go, and I won't kill you."

Trace snarled, his lip curling in an ugly sneer. He twisted the knife in his hand, pushing the tip into Serena's chin, a bead of blood appearing and sliding down the blade. Serena winced, a strangled cry escaping her.

"Fuck. You," Trace repeated.

A wave of nausea washed over Van, and black spots darkened his vision. He clenched his fists, his blunt nails digging into the palms of his hands. His throat constricted, and he couldn't get enough air.

Not again. He would not lose the woman he loved to another asshole. Not this time.

"Soldier. *Aanval.*"

The dog launched himself across the room, sinking his teeth into Trace's calf, clamping down tight. Trace screamed and stumbled back, releasing Serena and falling on his ass, the knife bouncing off the tile floor. Serena shoved herself away from him and tried to crawl to Van.

Trace kicked at Soldier, his steel-toed boot connecting with the dog's side, his hand landing on Serena's leg, holding tight. Soldier yelped, released Trace for a brief second, but he immediately latched back on. Serena ripped her leg free of Trace's grip, scrambled to her feet, and lunged at Van. At least he *thought* she was lunging at him.

Serena snatched the knife off the floor, turned around, and stabbed Trace in the upper thigh. He screamed and grabbed his leg, blood flowing from the wound, over his hands, and all over the kitchen floor.

"Soldier, *ophouden!*" Van shouted.

Soldier released Trace, but he stayed where he was, teeth bared, growling at Trace. Serena threw herself at Van, her arms around his neck, her face buried against his shoulder. Van pulled his gun from the waistband of his jeans and pointed it at Trace. With the other hand, he took his phone from his pocket and pushed it into Serena's hands.

"Call 911, sweetheart. Tell Sheriff Willis to hurry. And tell her we need an ambulance."

— *Van* —

Sheriff Donna Willis was swift and efficient. She took statements from Van and Serena while the paramedics worked on Trace. When they loaded him in the ambulance, she climbed in beside him, read him his rights, and handcuffed him to the gurney. Van wasn't sure how much of it Trace understood; they'd drugged him to help with his pain. If Van could have had his way, he would have left him to suffer.

"Ms. Chasey, how are you?" Sheriff Willis asked when she returned to the house.

"I'm fine," Serena replied. She sat in one of her dining room chairs, staring out the picture window, Soldier beside her, her fingers twisted in his fur. The dog refused to leave her side.

Sheriff Willis didn't look convinced. She crouched in front of Serena and put her hand on her knee. "I want you to go to the hospital."

"I said I was fine," Serena insisted.

"She'll go," Van interrupted. "I'll make sure of it."

Sheriff Willis smiled at him, but she didn't move. "Will you go?"

Serena nodded. A tear slid down her cheek and she absentmindedly wiped it away. She held her hand out to Van, who took it. She held it so tight her knuckles were white. "Thank you, Sheriff Willis. I really appreciate everything."

The sheriff rose to her feet and shook Van's hand. "I'll be in touch."

Serena waited until everyone had cleared out before she spoke. "Take me to your place? I can't be here." Her eyes darted to the blood on the floor then back to him. "Please?"

Van put his keys in her hand. "Take Soldier and go to my house. I'll pack you some stuff. You can stay as long as you want."

"I-I can't." Serena shook her head, her hair flying around her head. "I don't want to be by myself."

Van grabbed her shoulders and forced her to look at him. "You won't be alone. Soldier will take care of you. If anything happens, say his name and *aanval*. It means attack. Say it, sweetheart."

"*Aanval*," she whispered.

Soldier's ears twitched, but he didn't move until Serena rose to her feet, then he followed her, staying right by her side. She walked past Van in a daze, the tips of her fingers brushing Soldier's fur, the defeated sorrow on her face breaking Van's heart, then she disappeared out the door. He stood at the window watching her as she climbed the stairs and entered his condo. He saw the light come on and watched as she sat on the couch. Soldier jumped up and sat beside her.

He went to her room, grabbed a duffel bag from the closet, and threw some clothes in it. He stopped in the bathroom and threw her toiletries in as well. If he forgot anything, he would come over here and get it for her. Before he left, he called Clint, the maintenance guy.

"Mr. Brooks, how are you?" Clint said.

"I'm good, Clint. I have a favor to ask you." He explained what had happened and asked if Clint could get some cleaners in to clean the place up. Clint promised to get it taken care of right away.

Van slammed the door closed behind him and hurried across the street to his place. He put Serena's things

— *Van* —

upstairs, then he helped her into her coat, put Soldier's vest and leash on him, and loaded them into his truck.

The hospital was near the university; it took them less than fifteen minutes to get there. Sheriff Willis must have given them a heads up because they ushered Serena right back, the nurse ordering Van and Soldier to stay put. He did as he was told, but he wasn't happy about it and neither was Soldier. The dog whined and stared at the door Serena had gone through until Van scolded him.

"Soldier, *ga liggen. Komen*!"

The dog dropped to the floor, chuffing loudly, his focus on the door. At least he stayed quiet.

An hour later, Serena came out the door, a bandage on her chin where Trace had cut her, a small white bag clutched in her hand. Van rose to his feet and she threw herself into his arms, her head resting on his chest.

"Take me home."

Epilogue

Three Weeks Later

Serena threw another log on the fire and picked up the box of ornaments. She wanted to get the tree decorated before Van returned. He wouldn't tell her where he went or what he was doing; he'd kissed her goodbye, jumped in his truck, and left.

She'd taken advantage of the opportunity to pull the tree and decorations from the trunk of her car and drag them in the house. She rearranged the furniture and set up the five-foot tree in front of the window. It wasn't even Thanksgiving yet—not for another three days—but she wanted to surprise Van. When she'd mentioned putting up a tree earlier in the week, he'd sheepishly admitted he didn't have any decorations.

"Decorating for the holidays was Adelaide's thing." He shrugged. "After she died—"

Serena had silenced him with a kiss, her fingers in his hair, tugging him close. The pain they'd both suffered over the years was too much, unbearable and unfair. She was determined to move past it, to help Van move past it. While she knew she could never replace Adelaide, she could love him in her own way. She planned to do it until the day she died.

She put the last of the decorations on the tree and plugged it in. It was perfect; the reflection off the window was better than she'd expected. She couldn't wait for Van to see it.

"What do you think, Soldier?"

The dog didn't move; he was sacked out on the floor in front of the fire.

She laughed and glanced out the window at her condo across the street. She'd been back over there to grab some clothes and clean out the fridge before returning to Van's. Despite Clint cleaning the place up and replacing her door, she couldn't go back. She could smell the blood and hear Trace's voice in her head as soon as she stepped inside. She didn't feel safe there anymore.

Van hadn't protested, not even a little, when she moved herself into his place. It had been a simple transition; she fit into his life so easily it was like he'd been holding a place for her. Not that they'd made anything official. She just never went home.

Serena finished decorating the tree, then she put the boxes downstairs in the basement. She put a roast in the oven for dinner and poured herself a glass of wine. All she had left to do was hang up the stockings—one for Van, one for her, and one for Soldier. She placed the holders on

— *Epilogue* —

the mantel and hung them up, stepping back to see how they looked.

Pleased with what she'd accomplished, she sat down, pulled a blanket over her lap, and picked up her book. She managed to read a couple of pages before she heard the garage open and Van pull the truck inside.

He came up the stairs, his cheeks ruddy from the cold, a backpack slung over his shoulder. He stopped on the last step, a ghost of a smile on his lips. Serena pushed the blanket off her lap and rose to her feet, twisting her hands together as she tried to gauge his reaction.

"You've been busy," he murmured.

"Do you like it? I wanted to surprise you."

Van nodded. "It's beautiful. You did an amazing job. Come here."

She hurried around the couch and into Van's open arms. He pressed a kiss to her forehead and hugged her close.

"I have a surprise for you, too." He released her, tossed his backpack on the table, and shucked off his jacket. "I had a meeting with Charlie."

Serena stiffened, her eyes narrowing. "Why?"

"You are looking at the new head of campus security. Well, technically, B & D Protection Services is contracting with the university to provide security. I'll be overseeing it." He grinned. "But only if it's okay with you. I swear to God I'm not doing this to keep an eye on you or anything. I don't want you to think that. Me and Charlie talked about it a few weeks ago, a couple days after his party. I told him I had to think about it, though I was fairly certain I was gonna take it. My only condition is you sign off on it."

"Hm, would we be working together?"

"Not really. Charlie is giving me free reign to run things as I see fit, so I might see you if I have to meet with him." Van's grin faded away as he cleared his throat and shifted from foot to foot. "I won't take it if you don't want me there, sweetheart."

She cut him off, her mouth on his, her tongue dancing over his lips. "Can I at least steal you away for lunch once in a while?" she teased.

Van relaxed, the tension draining out of him. "I'd be upset if you didn't." He wrapped an arm around her waist and pulled her flush against his body. "There is something else we need to talk about."

"Okay." Serena drew the word out, wondering what else Van was up to. "What is it?"

"Your living situation." When Serena tried to pull away, Van held her tight, refusing to let her go. "I like having you here, sweetheart. A lot. I think we should make it permanent. What do you think?"

Her answer was a kiss that left them both panting. When they broke apart, her entire body was burning with need for Van.

"I'm gonna take that as a yes," he chuckled.

"It's definitely a yes," Serena breathed.

Van rested his forehead against hers. "Welcome home."

About the Author

I'm a northern girl who transplanted herself to the much warmer southwest thirty years ago, and I have no intention of ever going back. After all, you don't have to shovel sunshine. I've always been a voracious reader and ever since I was a little girl, I've had some kind of story playing in my head, daydreams that I turned into intricate stories. It took me forty-two years to put pen to paper and start writing, but I haven't looked back since. After my three children grew up and started their own lives, I decided it was time to chase my dreams. I've been running after them ever since.

I love writing contemporary, romantic erotica. I think it's fun to write people letting themselves go and getting down and dirty with someone that makes their blood boil. It's also my little secret - I might be innocent looking on the outside, but I'm a crazy smut writer on the inside. I stumbled into writing romantic erotica when I started writing fanfiction for my favorite obsessions. People seemed to love the smut, so I grabbed the reins and barreled headlong into writing it. One of my favorite series is JR Ward's Black Dagger Brotherhood series. I long to have people love my books like I love hers. She is an inspiration to me and my writing.

When I'm not busy writing, I love to binge-watch new shows, fawn over my favorite Supernatural monster hunters, rewatch my collection of Marvel movies, crochet, and spend time with my husband of twenty-seven years and our dogs.

Nothing makes me happier than readers becoming invested in my characters and my stories. I want to give readers an escape, a chance to get away from their everyday lives and be transported into a world of romance.

You can find me at mimifranciswriter.com or over on Twitter at @author_mimi.

Mimi Francis is a northern girl who transplanted herself to the much warmer southwest thirty years ago and has no intention of ever going back. After all, you don't have to shovel sunshine. She has always been a voracious reader and ever since she was a little girl, she had some kind of story playing in her head, daydreams that she turned into intricate stories. It took her forty-two years to put pen to paper and start writing, but she hasn't looked back since. After her three children grew up and started their own lives, she decided it was time to chase her dreams. She's been running after them ever since.

She loves writing contemporary, romantic erotica because she finds it fun to write people letting themselves go and getting down and dirty with someone that makes their blood boil. It's also her little secret - she might be innocent looking on the outside, but she's a crazy smut writer on the inside. Mimi stumbled into writing romantic

— About The Author —

erotica when she started writing fanfiction for her favorite obsessions. People seemed to love the smut, so she grabbed the reins and barreled headlong into writing it. One of Mimi's favorite series is JR Ward's Black Dagger Brotherhood series. Her dream is to have people love her books like she loves those. She is an inspiration to Mimi and her writing.

When she's not busy writing, Mimi loves to binge-watch new shows, fawn over her favorite Supernatural monster hunters, rewatch her collection of Marvel movies, crochet, and spend time with her husband of twenty-seven years and their dogs.

Nothing makes her happier than readers becoming invested in her characters and her stories. Mimi wants to give readers an escape, a chance to get away from their everyday lives and be transported into a world of romance.

You can find her at mimifranciswriter.com or over on Twitter at @author_mimi.

mimifrancis.com

Facebook.com/author.mimi.francis

INSTAGRAM: @author.mimi.francis

TWITTER: @author_mimi

4 Horsemen Publications

Romance

Ann Shepphird
The War Council

Emily Bunney
All or Nothing
All the Way
All Night Long
All She Needs
Having it All
All at Once
All Together
All for Her

Mimi Francis
Private Lives
Second Chances
Run Away Home
The Professor

Cozy Mysteries

Ann Shepphird
Destination: Maui
Destination: Monterey

4HorsemenPublications.com

www.ingramcontent.com/pod-product-compliance
Lightning Source LLC
LaVergne TN
LVHW041640060526
838200LV00040B/1654